FINDING MY DESTYNEE

RAFTER O RANCH BOOK THREE

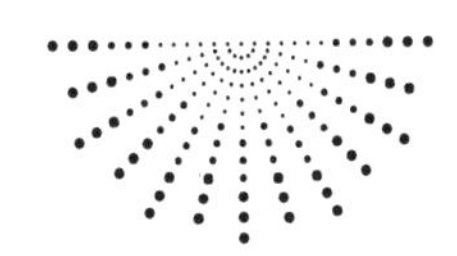

NATALIE BRIGHT
DENISE F. MCALLISTER

Finding My Destynee
Paperback Edition

CKN Christian Publishing
An Imprint of Wolfpack Publishing
9850 S. Maryland Parkway, Suite A-5 #323
Las Vegas, Nevada 89183

cknchristianpublishing.com

Print ISBN 978-1-63977-500-2
eBook ISBN 978-1-63977-914-7
LCCN 2022946483

FINDING MY DESTYNEE

"I will sing a new song to you, my God."

~Psalm 144:9 NIV

1
TRAVIS

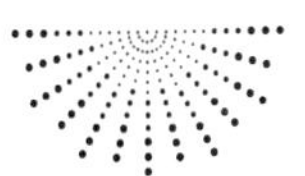

RAFTER O RANCH—DIXON, TEXAS

27 DAYS UNTIL CHRISTMAS

TRAVIS OLSEN KILLED ANOTHER SHOT OF tequila and stared out the front window at the weather-worn house across the street. Not much of a view. Not much of a life. So, what else is new? He let the empty bottle drop to the floor, extended the recliner and leaned further back, closing his eyes. Even with a good buzz from alcohol, his wife's face floated in his mind in full clarity. Every day. Every night. Nothing wiped it away.

A light knock on the front door occurred at the same time it swung open.

"Travis. It's Mom." Grace Olsen breezed into the room. "He took his first steps!"

Her cheeks were red from the cold, and she carried a bundle wrapped in a puffy coat and wool cap that was actually a child. His child. She sat him down on the floor and gently removed the coat. "Show Daddy, sweetheart."

"Good grief, Mother. Could you find any more clothes to put on him? He can hardly breathe." Even with his observation he didn't help his mother with the disrobing.

Finally, a smiling face appeared from the billowing cold weather gear.

"Dada," he said as he held out chubby fingers.

No matter how bad life sucked, this kid was always happy. He was too young to know that his own mother had abandoned him to chase her dreams. And too young to know that it was entirely his own father's fault.

Travis's mom's disapproving glance went from the bottle of tequila on the floor to his face. "It's Monday morning, for heaven's sake. You might try starting the week on a sober note."

He cringed but didn't care anymore. Grace Olsen had a knack for making him feel like the scum of the earth, and she did it in such a sweet, soft motherly voice.

He shrugged. "It was a rough weekend. We wore out some rodeo stock at Cody's and I'm just trying to get over the aches and pains."

And his physical condition was the least of his worries. She had never had to deal with anything like what his life had become. No one should have to face the cards he had been dealt.

Destynee. The name said it all. The love of his life deserted her husband and child, and the sad thing was he had encouraged her to leave. At the time, Travis thought it was the right thing to do. Now he realized how stupid the idea had been. But there was no going back. The kid's mother was going to be a big star.

In his solitary life he had mulled it over and over a thousand ways to Sunday and still came up with the same answer. How could he not let her go? How could he stand in the way of her following the dream? She had a God-given talent. How could he cover that up and make her stay? They had talked about it very briefly and vowed to make it work. But now it had been weeks and weeks. How many—he had lost count. And their boy was growing like a rambunctious colt.

Wyatt dropped to his bottom on the floor and stared at his father.

"Stand up. Show Daddy what you did this morning." Grace urged the toddler on but he ignored her. He stared up with those big, blue eyes. The same eyes as his mother's.

Truth be known, Travis didn't resent his wife as much as he did her mother, Julee Rae. A wannabe country singer who never made it was now pushing her daughter to chase after the dream. He tried to like his mother-in-law, but she sure made it difficult. He still cringed when he remembered Destynee's mane of startling red-tinted hair only two days before their wedding. Conveniently, it had matched Julee Rae's red-dyed locks. What happened to the gorgeous blonde-haired bride that Travis had loved since junior high school? It was obvious that Destynee was only trying to please her mother; the mother who had been plotting and manipulating her daughter's whole life.

As much as his own mother was bugging him lately, he was grateful to have her instead of Julee Rae. Grace was always there for her children. He should thank her, but he was in such a low place he couldn't find any thanks in his heart right now.

"Mom, I'm not feeling so great. Can you watch Wyatt again today? I need to find the aspirin."

"Seems to me like you haven't been feeling well for a long time now, Travis. You know I'll always help you. But your son is starting to walk. You've got to get a hold of yourself and be a father. He needs you."

She wasn't telling him anything he didn't already know.

Wyatt scooted closer to Travis with a wide, gurgling smile. When he got to the chair, he reached and grabbed his daddy's pant leg. Using everything he could muster, with a grunt and red face to match, he pulled himself up to sway on unsteady legs. The wide grin never left his face.

"Good boy," said Grace. "Now come here, Wyatt. Show your daddy what you did this morning."

Wyatt twisted his upper body to look at his grandmother, but his lower body stayed planted. He reached up one hand to his father. Travis picked him up and sat him on his lap.

"Hey, little man." Travis kissed him on his head which made the tyke giggle. Those blue eyes. That grin. Just like his mother. Travis had fallen for Destynee the first moment he saw her riding a strawberry roan mare into the arena at a local high school rodeo. She had blonde hair that reached her waist and big blue eyes the same color of the sparkling shirt she wore, a hat to match, and red boots. The horse was giving her problems, but she managed to handle the reins and hang on to the Texas flag that she carried. He would remember that image until his last breath, and her name would be the last word he uttered.

Travis should've been happy and proud to be holding their son but looking at Wyatt only made the resentment worse. He couldn't help but think about all the pieces of their life Destynee was missing. He stood Wyatt back down on the floor.

"This way, Wyatt." Grace gave him a wide grin. "You can do it."

Wyatt took one step, then hesitated. Took another

wobbly step and then two more which placed him in the middle of the room without his father's leg for support. He looked at his father. He turned his head to look at his grandmother. As if realizing the predicament he was in, he screwed up his face, planted flat on his bottom, and let out a long squall.

Travis grabbed his head. "Mother, you've got to take him, and I need something for this headache." The sadness in Grace's eyes made Travis feel lower than a snake. He wouldn't win any parenting awards, that's for sure.

"We'll go then." Grace gathered up Wyatt's outerwear as Travis disappeared into the bathroom to search for anything to cut the edge off the pounding in his head. When he got back to the living room, he was alone. So, what else is new?

2
DESTYNEE

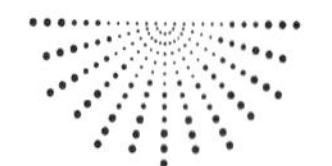

26 DAYS UNTIL CHRISTMAS

"MOTHER, WILL WE HAVE TIME FOR DINNER before the concert tonight? I'm hungry. Aren't you? We didn't have much of a breakfast and we skipped lunch to rehearse."

"I'm fine. I had a power bar earlier. You'd better wait until after. You don't want to be bloated. Or burp onstage, for heaven's sake. Have some gum or a mint." Julee Rae was looking closely into the mirror as she spoke, carefully positioning a set of black false eyelashes onto her lids. Even with a few extra pounds gained over the years, she was an attractive woman and she dressed the part of someone who was always in the public eye. Head to toe, nothing out of place, and she expected the same standards for her only daughter. Her natural hair color was dark brown whereas Destynee was a natural blonde, but the color of Julee Rae's could change on a whim depending if she had a new outfit. Today she had chosen a more business casual ensemble.

"You look nice, Mom." Destynee checked the time. Three hours, almost four, till show time. She wasn't sure she'd make it. Her stomach grumbled its agreement.

"Now remember, I was able to book two performances for us in West Plains. It's only about an hour from here. We can leave soon. I reserved another motel there. You go on at six o'clock at the Baptist church for their revival. A few worship-type songs. Eight o'clock appearance at the South Plains Mall. You're the headliner after the local drill team does their thing. Lots of people will be there doing their holiday shopping. I'll set your clothes out on the bed. And I got you some shapewear to hold in your gut."

Destynee looked down at her figure. She was a size two with barely a tummy, even after having baby Wyatt. She certainly wasn't obese or anything.

"Mother?"

Julee Rae strenuously teased her hair higher and kept talking. "And then the next day we have a bit of a drive to Cedar Mills for the Holiday Jamboree. They've invited you back again this year."

"Do you think we could…uh…go home after that?"

"Home? You mean Dixon? What's there for us in that nowhere little town?"

Destynee's eyes stared at her mother and began filling with tears, as hard as she fought to keep them at bay. "I miss Travis and Wyatt. I'd like to see my son, Mother."

"Wyatt is just fine. He's got that rich Olsen family to look out for him. They can afford whatever he needs. Do you really want to be changing smelly diapers now? Or do you want to be pursuing your dream? And then you'll be the one who gives Wyatt a better life. Don't you want a nice big house for him? Besides, Grace Olsen likes that sort of stuff—raising kids. So let her do it. Makes her happy."

"But, Mother, he's my son. I'm missing out on all his firsts. Teeth. Walking. Talking."

"Those are really no big things. Motherhood is overrated. Just think, you work hard, you make a lot of money, you go back, and Grace Olsen will have the boy walking and talking and you can then enjoy him. No dirty diapers. And he'll love all the toys you can buy him. The big house with the big yard. The pony. Everyone wins. You'll see. Trust your mama. Why don't you take a quick nap? Close your eyes for a while. I'll pack the car. Then we can get out of Odessa."

Destynee laid her head back on the pillow, the case was a dingy yellow rather than bright white. The cheap motels they had been staying in were giving her the creeps. In fact, sometimes she felt like bugs were crawling on her although she never actually saw one.

Her mind drifted to thoughts of having her own home, her husband, her son, even her own washing machine, doing the laundry, and hanging the sheets on the line in the Texas wind to dry. She wouldn't make her beds with dingy pillowcases. Maybe Wyatt would be outside with her in a playpen cooing and laughing in the sun. Travis would come home for lunch which she had ready and waiting for him. He'd give her a kiss as he reached around her waist and pulled her tight to his chest. They would laugh and kiss and play as happy young couples do.

And her mother would not be in the picture.

God forgive her for her selfish thoughts.

She had watched her mother for months, day after day, working really hard to find Destynee singing jobs. Julee Rae did everything for her—found her clothes they could afford, motels to stay in, musicians to accompany Destynee.

It was true. She wanted to be successful with her singing career. She loved singing and wanted to contribute to her and Travis's little family. Help Wyatt to grow up to be a happy, kind young man with all the opportunities he deserved. If that meant doing what her mother told her to do and following her advice, Destynee figured she could do it without complaint. Like any other job. One day at a time. One foot in front of the other. Like an obedient soldier. She would keep at it until the day she could return to her husband and child. Then, maybe, all her dreams would come true.

It seemed like only ten minutes had passed. "Destynee, come on. Better get up. You don't need puffy eyes."

"Let's get the car loaded. For tomorrow, I want you to wear the blue dress for the church. It's a little longer, to your knees. The little old church ladies will like it. And stick to what we rehearsed. "How Great Thou Art" and finish with "Amazing Grace". You can't go wrong with those two. Red sparkly mini dress for the mall and sing a happy tune that showcases your range. They won't forget you. That song by Melinda about "Gettin' Drunk". It's got a good drumbeat. And remember to shake your booty. The crowd will love that."

Destynee swung her legs off the side of the bed. "Mother, I'd like to pick some better songs. I've written a couple of new ones."

High-pitched laughter came out of Julee Rae's mouth and hit the ceiling causing a chill to move up Destynee's spine. "Don't be silly, Sweetheart. You can't do unknown songs. We've talked about that. How are the people gonna relate? It's got to be something familiar, something they can tap their foot to and sing along. Maybe someday you can play your own stuff. But not now. We're trying to get your career off the ground. Not drive it into the dirt."

Her mother's bright red lips resembled those of a circus clown and Destynee had to look away. She pulled her boots on, grabbed her jacket and a small tote, and headed for the door. She didn't pause to look in the mirror nor did she pay attention to the names and places her mother rambled on about. One more town, a different stage, another song to a crowd of strangers. What did it matter?

"I'm ready, Mother."

"Well, it's about time. We have a schedule to keep. I can't afford for you to become complacent. I signed my name on the dotted line for some of these appearances. My reputation is at stake if you keep making us late." With a loud *humpff* she grabbed her oversized carryall bag and opened the door. Destynee carried her guitar case and a small bag with the change of clothes to the car.

It wasn't the squeal of laughter that hurt as much as the look on her mother's face. A cold hint of mockery with a slight roll of the eyes, as if her daughter's music was too ridiculous to even consider. Destynee could no more stop the lyrics and melodies swirling in her head than she could stop the sun from coming up the next day. It was part of who she was, or wanted to be, as a performer and sometimes the songs came so fast it was like a thundering concert in her skull. Julee Rae had never encouraged it. Always willing to please and not cause trouble, Destynee did her best to tap it down. She kept silent. She did what she was told. But somedays she felt like she might explode.

3
TRAVIS

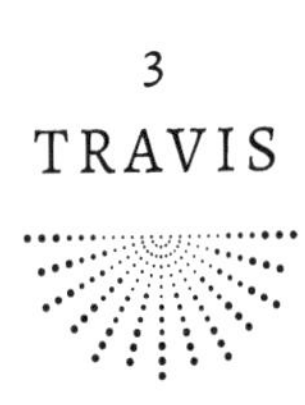

25 DAYS UNTIL CHRISTMAS

TRAVIS BUCKLED WYATT INTO HIS CAR SEAT. "Are you ready to go see Meme and Pappy?"

The promise to see his grandmother didn't erase the bottom lip stuck out in a pout or the pool of tears that rolled down his face. The reason for the meltdown had to do with a refusal to wear a blue shirt with a dog face versus the red shirt with a cow. The cow shirt was stained with dark dots of purple Kool-Aid and splotches of red spaghetti sauce. Despite his best efforts and constant advice from his mother, Travis let the toddler win this round. Again.

"That's enough, Wyatt. I need you to stop crying." He dug inside a fast-food sack to find an unused napkin and wiped his son's nose. The stiff napkin made Wyatt pull back and turn his head, leaving his nose blotchy and irritated.

Travis left the door open and ran back inside to get the diaper bag and did a mental checklist of everything he needed. The clothes he had stuffed inside the bag were dirty, too, but he couldn't help that. As a side note, he grabbed the bottle of aspirin for the headache he knew he would have later. He had successfully cut down on the whiskey last night because Wyatt filled every minute and took every ounce of energy he had left.

Bath, a long deliberation of which pajamas to wear, bedtime story no less than five times through the retelling, and prayers. They always said a prayer for Mama. That she'd be safe and that her singing would bring joy to all the people who came to see her perform. Wyatt didn't ask too many questions about her because he was so young and accepting of his life. But Travis knew better. Their life would be so much better just having her there. But his selfishness could drive her away forever. It wasn't his decision to keep her from the audiences. She should be sharing her gift with others. Yet the sting of resentment never left him, particularly when he looked at his son and saw those same blue eyes.

He backed out of the driveway of his wife's childhood home, irritation rising like bile in his throat every time he had to look at the front of the house. While Destynee and her mother were on the road, he was supposed to take care of the place. He paid the bills from a small account his mother-in-law had added his name to, but he barely had enough left for food and Wyatt's diapers. Thank goodness his mother and father had pitched in to help with their grandson.

For pocket money, he scored sometimes at several steer ropings and jackpot rodeos, if he could get an invitation, and also did odd day working jobs for area ranches. He was too proud to ask to be put on the payroll at the Rafter O. His sister would be his boss. Not that it bothered him, her being in charge. It was admitting to the world that he needed help.

After they were married, he had quickly agreed to live there with Destynee at her mother's insistence. Blinded by love obviously, because there was nothing in this house that reflected anything about his wife. It was all about his mother-in-law, even the bedroom he slept in now. The only thing she had done was decorate a nursery for Wyatt with a crib and toys, and even then, the fabric and curtains had colorful musical notes and rows of piano keys. Forty-five records embellished the walls along with plastic guitars. A black and white poster covered the space over the crib which read *Born to Make Noise*. The mobile hanging from the ceiling had musical notes and clouds.

In Destynee's room, the one he now used, the musical theme continued with photographs on the wall of Julee Rae and the famous country singers she had known in the early days of her career. There wasn't one photo of Destynee at any of her performances. Kind of strange, he thought. Right after their wedding and the birth of Wyatt, Destynee had been content to be a wife and mother, but she had a problem saying no. Julee Rae was a mighty force, and that force was focused one hundred and ten percent on her only child.

It wasn't long into their marriage that Julee Rae had Destynee back on the road. She used to call every night, but it had been two weeks since he'd last talked to his wife. He wanted to call and insist she be home for Christmas, but that was a month away so he waited. Thanksgiving had been a lonely time for him, sitting with his family while they all gushed over the two grandsons, Wyatt and his older brother's son, Gabe. Destynee was in Dallas singing at a megachurch for their Thanksgiving service the night before, and Julee Rae said she'd be too tired to make the drive back to Dixon the next day.

Travis had suffered through the day and drowned his sorrows that night. Wyatt's tears dried up as the motion of the vehicle caused him to doze. It was a silent ride out to the Rafter O Ranch headquarters. Travis was meeting several other cowboys there to spend the afternoon sharpening their team roping skills. His dad kept a dozen roping steers just for that purpose, and on occasion they were able to find an afternoon when they could get together. Travis wanted to enter the ranch rodeo next year, if he could find enough guys who were interested in forming a ranch team for the Rafter O.

ALL TEARS WERE FORGOTTEN the minute Grace leaned into the vehicle to unbuckle Wyatt. Travis was thankful that his mother and his son had formed such a strong bond. On the other hand, it made him even sadder that Destynee wasn't home to know her child.

They had produced the most amazing kid Travis had ever known in his life. Smart, hilariously funny, and the spittin' image of his mother. She was missing out on so much of her lively little son.

"There's my precious boy," Grace said as she lifted Wyatt from the car seat. "Tell Daddy to do good. You boys have fun."

Of course, Wyatt never gave his father a second glance; all eyes were for his grandmother. He ruffled his son's hair and gave a quick smile to his mother before getting his rope and walking to the barn to find his father.

"Mornin'." Travis looped the rope around the neck of his gelding.

His father nodded. His brother Nathan pulled up with his friend Colton in the passenger seat. Within several more minutes, Lank from the neighboring Wild Cow Ranch arrived pulling a livestock trailer. He waved his hand as he stepped out of his pickup truck, and then unloaded his horse.

While the cowboys saddled up, Skip Olsen turned the roping steers into a small alleyway which had a chute at one end. The men worked to fasten horn wraps on every steer's head which offered protection to the horns and head of the animal.

The first team up for roping was Travis and Lank. They had worked together before, with Lank heading and Travis as heeler. On one side of the corral, they had a small chute with a closure and lever. The roping team called "Ready" and Colton pulled the lever. The calf shot out like a rocket. The header successfully cast a loop around the horns to swing the animal around so that the back feet were in a direct line with Travis as he came up from behind. He let his loop fly and snagged both back feet. Done. The calf successfully stretched out between them. Travis swung off his horse and loosened the rope.

The men took turns over the next several hours, trading off partners and switching from heading to heeling. A good day's work of practice. The calves gathered at one end of the arena and they all rode towards them.

"That one there has a bit of a runny nose. We may need to doctor him." Skip steered his horse in that direction as he swung a loop over his head. He let it fly aiming for the back two legs. The rope caught but before it stretched taut, another solid muscled calf ran straight into the rope, tried to jump, and snagged his front hoof on the rope instead. An expert horseman, Skip tried to stop his horse and steer him in the direction of the tangled steers, but the momentum had them all in motion. The steers went one way and the horse moved in backward motion. There was only one victor and the weight of the steers won out, dragging the horse off balance and to the ground with Skip along with him.

4
TRAVIS

ALL FOUR COWBOYS BOUNDED OFF THEIR horses in a flash running towards Skip Olsen who was pinned under his horse. Lank produced a pocket knife and sliced the rope. It trailed behind the calves as they shot towards the far corner of the arena. Travis and Nathan were quickly at their dad's side. Colton went to the head of the horse.

"He's out cold," Nathan said. "Call an ambulance."

"I'll hold the horse still if y'all can pull him out from under." Colton grabbed the reins and put a hand on the horse's head. The animal's eyes were wide and fearful. "Easy, fella."

Each brother grabbed an arm and gently pulled Skip out from under his horse.

"Did you call?" Nathan's voice punched the air in a panic.

"I will," said Travis.

"Maybe we should get him in my truck," Lank offered.

"If the air ambulance isn't in use, it'll get here much faster." Nathan was in leader mode.

Travis punched the numbers and the emergency operator took the information. "Helicopter is on the way."

"You have to go tell Mom." Nathan looked at Travis.

"I'm not leaving him." He shook his head.

"I'm not leaving either," said Colton.

Travis placed a finger on his father's throat. He could barely feel a pulse, faint but it was there. His father's face was relaxed, peaceful even. Travis's heart felt like it was going to explode and he couldn't find any air, but he forced himself to remain calm. Yes, somebody should run to the house and tell his mother, but he was too afraid to take his hands off his father's shoulder. He wanted to be there in case he woke up.

With worried frowns, they kneeled in the dirt beside Skip. Travis hurried to the shed, jumped into the four-wheeler and shot towards the front yard, his eyes on the sky, his ears straining for the familiar *thwap* and engine of the air ambulance. Familiar because it hadn't been that long ago the chopper had landed at Rafter O headquarters for Skip who had collapsed during Travis's wedding. Something to do with his heart. Thank God they hadn't lost him then.

While he waited, he pulled his phone out to contact his mother. A phone call seemed wrong. A text seemed even worse, but he couldn't leave. He just rang her number. "Dad has had an accident. We've already called for the chopper."

He heard a gasp, the clatter of a dropped phone, and the sight of his mother running out of the house immediately towards the corral.

Travis heard the helicopter before he saw it, and then suddenly it appeared like a dot on the horizon. He knew they were traveling fast, but it seemed like it took ages before they landed in the pasture at the side of the house. He waved. Travis gunned the four-wheeler and was parked next to the chopper by the time the medics' feet hit the ground. They were the same guys who handled the last incident. One tall blonde and tan, like he should have a surfboard under his arm instead of a medic bag. He quickly stuck out his hand.

"I'm Jason. You're Travis, right? This is our paramedic in charge, Rob." He nodded towards the other man who jumped out of the air ambulance.

"We understand there has been an accident involving Mr. Olsen?" The other medic was the exact opposite in looks with long black braids that fell on either side of his dark face. His dark eyes showed genuine concern.

"Yes, hop in. I'll take you to where he is." They loaded the gurney into the back. Travis didn't waste any time to even see if they were holding on. He gunned the ATV and shot out across the pasture towards the arena.

Travis suddenly felt relief. Both men were extremely capable at their jobs. They had saved his father's life once before. No question.

The men didn't talk again as they squatted on either side of their still unconscious patient. The other cowboys backed away to give them room to work, but Grace stayed kneeling on the ground next to Skip.

"Mr. Olsen. Can you open your eyes?" Deep frowns of concern appeared on both their faces.

The medics strapped Skip to the gurney and with painstaking care started rolling him out of the arena and across the yard to the helicopter.

Travis stood there, helpless and useless. The sight of his father so motionless and still was a shock. Nathan took charge.

"I'll call Indya and have her get a hold of that babysitter down the road. She can watch both boys. She knows Gabe from a couple of times we brought him. Mother, if they let you, ride with Dad on the helicopter. Travis, you need to head towards the hospital now, and you might contact Angie. Have you seen her? Tell her to call Janie and try to get a message to Libbie at college."

Travis followed behind his older brother, still at a loss for words and too stunned to make sense of what he was supposed to be doing. Please God, give the medical team steady hands and knowledgeable minds. We're not ready for you to take Dad home.

5
DESTYNEE

24 DAYS UNTIL CHRISTMAS

DESTYNEE LET THE HOT WATER POUND HER face. At least they had a hot water heater. Typical of her mother to save money, several of the dive motels they had stayed in before couldn't even provide a hot shower. When Destynee turned the water off, she heard her phone buzzing. She reached around the shower curtain to wrap a towel around her body, held it with one hand and picked up her phone, which was on the counter. In the tiny bathroom she didn't have to even step out of the shower to answer it. "Hello."

"Destynee? This is Angie Olsen."

Her breath caught in her throat. Travis. Wyatt. Please God, let them be all right.

"Is everyone okay?"

"Oh, yes. I didn't mean to scare you. Travis and Wyatt are fine. It's my dad. He had a serious horse wreck and hasn't come out of a coma yet. He's in ICU at the medical center in Amarillo. I just wanted you to know.

Travis would have called, but the guys were roping when it happened and he's still shaken up. I got elected to notify everyone."

"I am sorry to hear that. Thanks for calling me." She stepped into the room and sank to one end of the only bed. Her knees were wobbly but relief flooded her mind. She couldn't suppress the whoosh of air that left her.

"I figured you would want to know. Please keep him in your prayers."

"I'll do that." An awkward silence hung in the air between them for several seconds.

"Are your shows going all right?"

"Yes, everything seems to be running smoothly thanks to my mother. Tell Travis and Wyatt I said hello." She paused and realized how rude that may seem. "And tell everyone hello."

"Yes, I will. See ya soon, maybe."

Julee Rae swung the door open and stepped into the room like a whirling dervish. She froze in her tracks.

"Maybe so. Thanks again for calling." Destynee ended the call and placed her phone on the bed.

"Who was that?" Julee Rae asked as she piled sacks into the one and only chair in the room.

"Angie Olsen."

"What did she want?"

"Skip had a horse accident. He's in the ICU."

"Sorry to hear that." She began opening the bags. "I need you to try this on. It might work for one of your performances. It's a big stage and the audience sits far away. I want you in something bright and glittery so they can see you. I also found this dress that will work for Saturday's chili cook off, but I want you to wear your boots."

Destynee barely glanced at the clothing, slipping back

into the bathroom instead and closing the door behind her. On her phone she pulled up a map, but the name of the town they were in suddenly escaped her. She had been in so many the past few months, she had grown numb as to where they were going. Her mother kept talking from the other side of the closed door. Destynee blocked her voice out, as usual. She didn't care where they were going, she just wanted to get it done. The sooner the dates were checked off, the sooner she could go home.

She admitted to being a bit technically challenged. She spent every spare second playing her music instead of being online, but she remembered seeing a map on her mother's phone that had a dot for the location. Julee Rae had asked her to help navigate through a congested downtown area one time. Why didn't her phone have a dot? She went into Settings. Location. Allow. That had to be it. A gasp of surprise escaped her lips. She wouldn't be that far from Amarillo on Friday, the night of the jamboree. She opened the bathroom door.

"I think I should go."

"Of course, you're going. Now hurry up and get dressed."

"No, I mean to the hospital."

"That's ridiculous. You can't make it back in time for your set at the jamboree. As for tonight, we need to leave in a few minutes. They have you set up for sound check right after noon."

"It's a big stage with lots of performers scheduled. They won't miss me. I can leave for Amarillo and be back in time for the chili cook off the next day. Isn't it in the next town over? What, thirty miles or so?"

"You're not going anywhere near that hospital. That's final." She frowned. A flush crept up Julee Rae's neck to her face. "Now get dressed. I need to check my emails and send a fax. I hope this hotel has a business center or something."

Julee Rae left in the same cloud of stressful energy she had appeared in, leaving Destynee sitting on the bed still wrapped in a towel. With a heavy sigh she fell back on the mattress. She was a wife and a mother, and she was sharing a room and a bed with her difficult mother. The same life she had lived since as long as she could remember. She supposed there had been a father in her life at some point, but she couldn't remember him and her mother never mentioned a husband.

When she was elementary school age her mother entered her in local pageants. She could still rub her head and feel the pain of Julee Rae yanking and teasing her baby fine blonde hair into a poufy hairdo and jabbing the combs of a dime store tiara into her tender scalp. Junior high and high school were the same. Julee Rae used to tell her, "Baby, you've got to use this time when you're young and beautiful. Nobody's gonna want you when you're old and flabby. Trust me. I know."

Destynee got dressed, and deep down not accepting defeat just yet. There had to be a way.

For once she needed to think about her new family, and part of her family was her father-in-law. The father of her husband. Destynee wanted desperately to drive to Dixon to be there in support of her husband, stop by the hospital and let the Olsens know she was praying for his recovery. She could at least do that much. There had to be a way.

6
DESTYNEE

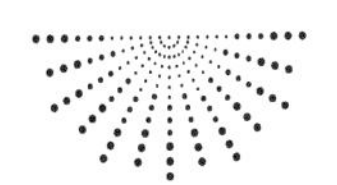

At the small white church Destynee closed her eyes and let her voice soar from the red carpeted altar to the sturdy rafters she was sure had been cut by the saws of the townsfolk decades ago. When she came to the end of her song, she saw many damp eyes and some with actual tears on the congregation's faces. They had been moved by her singing. And that's all she ever wanted. To connect with her audience and touch their hearts.

Later in the fellowship hall member after member approached her for an autograph, a selfie, a hug, or any combination of the three. They all told her, "You were amazing! What a gift from God. You have the voice of an angel. Thank you for coming to our church."

Some added, "Have some meatballs. Or a piece of coconut cake. You must be hungry."

She was. But she knew they had to leave any minute to make it to the mall. And she had to change dresses.

Her mother suddenly appeared at her side with a tote bag.

"Here. Run into that bathroom and change. Don't let the church folks see you in the short dress. Wrap a jacket around the bottom if you have to. I've already said our thank yous and goodbyes. They gave us a love offering of a hundred dollars. Better than nothing. I'll move the car around to the back-parking lot. Just duck out that door and meet me. And don't dawdle."

"Yes, Mother."

As Julee Rae disappeared out the door, Destynee's stomach roared loudly and she put a hand on it. She was so close to the food table. What would a few bites hurt? She needed something to hold her for the next few hours.

Looking around she only saw a couple of ladies straightening the table. Other guests were already chowing down on their overflowing plates in the side room where there were tables and chairs.

One of the elderly ladies approached. "I made these myself." She handed her a paper plate stacked high with the flakiest cream puffs she had ever seen. Destynee scanned the room like a criminal.

"Thank you." She smiled at the lady and took the plate.

As Destynee stood next to the table of treats, still perusing the options after the lady left, something touched her ankle. She jumped a little and when she looked down, a little boy peeked out from under the white tablecloth and giggled.

"Oh, my," she said. "Who are you? And what are you doing under there?"

His mouth full, he said, "Hidin'. And eatin'."

His face was covered with powder and his little hand held a big, white donut with sprinkles.

"I see," she said. "Where's your mother?"

"Dunno," he mumbled. "In there." He pointed to the side room where people were eating at tables.

"How old are you?" Destynee asked as she bent down to his level. She hoped her own mother would take a while so she could visit with this cutie a minute longer.

He held up five fingers. "My birthday was last Saturday. I had a dinosaur cake."

"That must've been fun," she said. "I have a little boy, too. But he's not even two yet."

The little guy looked up at her with bulging eyes. "Does he sing?"

"Hmmm, I'm not sure yet. Do you sing?"

"Sure do." He was a confident little guy. Suddenly he started singing a few stanzas of "Jesus Loves Me, This I Know."

She was amazed at the strength of his voice and that he knew all the words. When he was done, she clapped lively and said, "That was great. I really liked it. But I've got to go now. Thanks so much for singing for me. I hope to see you again one day."

The boy stared at her, then gave her a giant smile and said, "You're pretty."

Her heart was about to burst so she quickly ducked into the restroom, locked the door, and set down her tote. Staring into the cracked mirror, then to the plate of five creampuffs covered with white air-filled frosting. Before she knew it, three were stuffed in her mouth. Then the last two. Her lips were smeared with the evidence.

An authoritative knock sounded on the door. "Destynee! Are you in there? We've got to hurry. What are you doing?" The doorknob rattled.

She swallowed frantically and wiped her mouth with a rough brown paper towel.

"Mmm, hmmm. Be out in a minute, Mother."

"Well, hurry."

Destynee crinkled the paper plate and shoved it to the bottom of the wastebasket. She pulled the red dress on and tied a jacket around her waist to cover any indecency. Grabbing the tote, she flung open the door to find her mother on her way out of the building's side door, but close enough to turn back around and look at her daughter.

"What happened to your lipstick? You're gonna have to fix your face before we get to the mall. Hurry up and get in the car before anyone sees you."

"Yes, Mother." She always obeyed. Yet her thoughts were filled with the little boy she had just met. And her little boy that she had left at home. When would she see him?

THE MALL PERFORMANCE didn't go as well as the revival. The noise level drowned out her guitar, and the sound system was antiquated. She gave it her all, but hardly anyone stopped their shopping long enough to listen.

Back at the motel, Julee Rae insisted on making Destynee a cup of hot lemon tea and honey with strict instructions not to talk. Their conversations usually turned to arguing resulting in an apology and her mother getting her way. Destynee was okay with not talking. It gave her time to think.

Skip had been on her mind all day. She worried about Travis and Grace. She worried about all of them really and it frustrated her not knowing any details. If only she could talk to Travis.

She sipped the hot tea, sitting on the edge of a faded vinyl chair and waiting for her mother to do something besides lounging on the bed with her feet up flipping through channels on the television.

"I'd like to watch a good movie this evening." Julee Rae had never relaxed for one minute in her entire life, certainly never long enough to sit still for a two-hour movie. So why did she have to start now? And to make matters worse, Destynee felt like she had to slip her phone under one leg. Out of sight, out of mind. She didn't want her mother to suspect her of anything. To watch the two of them together, a person would never guess that Destynee had a husband and a son. Good grief, she still acted like a child.

"Do you need the bathroom before I take a shower?"

Destynee let out a huge sigh of relief. "No. I'm good."

After the water started running, she counted to ten and then pulled out the phone and tip-toed to the door. Very carefully to avoid her mother overhearing, she opened the door and slipped outside. Leaning on the railing she dialed Travis.

He answered immediately. "Destynee."

"How is your dad?"

"He's still unconscious, but there is good brain activity." His voice broke." We're keeping a close watch and a friend of Mom's organized a prayer vigil. Several of us go in to see him every two hours when visitation is allowed in the ICU. They only let two of us go at a time."

"I wish I could be there. I just wanted you to know that."

"I'm glad you called. It's good to hear your voice."

Destynee asked him what happened, but assured him he didn't have to talk about it. But he did want to talk about it. In fact, he talked and talked and time got away from her until her mother opened the hotel room door.

"Who are you talking to?"

She placed a hand over the speaker and glared at her mother, although the effort at intimidation was wasted. "My husband."

"You need to be asleep and out of this night air. It's not good for your vocal cords."

Destynee nodded. Travis had gone quiet. "I'm sorry. Mother wants me to come inside."

The line was silent for several minutes and she wondered if they had lost the connection.

"I love you," was the quiet reply.

"I love you, too. Keep me updated, okay?"

"I'll try. Gotta go. It's my turn to go in with Mom." The line went dead and suddenly Destynee felt completely alone and empty. She forgot to ask about Wyatt. Or maybe he avoided telling her about their son. If Grace was at the hospital and Travis was there, too, then who had Wyatt?

7
DESTYNEE

23 DAYS UNTIL CHRISTMAS

JULEE RAE WOKE DESTYNEE EARLY WITH instructions to carry their bags to the car. While her mother primped in the bathroom, Destynee became more frustrated, more impatient with each haul. The costumes were important but a monumental task to pack and unpack, plus her mother kept buying more in every town where they stopped. She had begun to hate the endless stream of sequined gowns, western shirts with fringe, belts, bracelets, hats, and shoes to match. Wear the boots. Don't wear the boots. By now, she had one entire suitcase of shoes and boots. Ridiculous. Destynee was to the point that she rarely cared what was covering her body, as long as it was covered, and as long as her guitar was slung over one shoulder.

Julee Rae drove them to the next town chattering nonstop. Destynee blocked her mother's voice with her ear buds but the phone in her pocket was silenced. She had to think about how she might get to the medical center in Amarillo.

There was no explanation for it, but she had an overwhelming desire to be there. She knew that Travis would be fretting. She had known Travis since grade school, dated him since high school, and he was a worrier. But he never complained or expressed his thoughts. He disappeared into a silent, empty world and stopped talking to everybody. She was the only one who could bring him out of that deep sadness. She certainly couldn't help Skip recover, but she could pray and be there at her husband's side.

The sense of her needing to be someplace else made her nauseated. Her mother's voice made her even more nervous. Julee Rae pulled into a convenience store to buy gas and then went inside to find food. Destynee waited until they were back on the road again, her mother happily munching on powdered doughnuts before she brought the subject up again.

"I tried to call Travis again, but he didn't answer." Lie, and then she wondered why she hadn't tried to contact him. "I wonder if Skip came out of his coma."

"He's not that young. He's lived a long life."

"Isn't he the same age as you?" Destynee glanced at her mother as two manicured pink nails carefully moved a powdery white bite in front of her mouth.

"He's lived a harder life. When your time is up, it's up."

She had never noticed her mother to be so callous and uncaring before.

"He's my father-in-law, Mother. The grandfather of my son. I really think that I should go visit him at the hospital." Destynee paused and then added very slowly.

"I can't be there every day, but I can support my husband."

"We have talked about this before and it is not up for discussion. My reputation is on the line if you're a no-show. Word would spread like a wild fire. I can't mend that type of damage. We are on a roll, baby. People are remembering you and your songs. They're inviting you back."

Destynee sighed. "How long will we have to do this?"

"As long as it takes. We go through every door that opens, and if necessary, we force it open. Whatever we have to do."

Destynee couldn't agree more. Whatever we have to do. Her priorities were changing. She felt a new door was about to open, but she wasn't sure if her mother would play as big a role. There would be a time when she'd have to find her own way, decide for herself the kind of life she wanted. There was more to that statement than she had ever realized.

She prayed that she'd be able to recognize the time when it was right.

DESTYNEE WAITED PATIENTLY backstage until her turn to sing. This holiday jamboree had been on her singing schedule since junior high, and they invited her back year after year. Her mother always accepted the invitation. Never once had she asked Destynee if she wanted to perform here or not. Tonight, she was diverting from the schedule a bit.

One song was all she had to get through, and then she would make her escape. She had thought about it all afternoon although she never had a chance to call Travis again. Exit on the opposite side of the stage from where her mother now stood. The car keys in her pocket were easy to keep after she insisted on driving to the venue. Her mother would stand backstage, hobnob and make connections long after Destynee finished her set. And she usually had a business dinner leaving her daughter to jam and rehearse with the band after the main performance in preparation for the next gig down the road.

The Amarillo Medical Center was only an hour and a half away. She'd probably be back to the arena before her mother even noticed she was gone. Thank goodness she had a spot early in the lineup.

The stage manager gave her the signal.

"Put your hands together to welcome a little lady all the way from Dixon, Texas. Say hello to Destynee!"

She walked out to sing a Patsy Cline favorite, "Walkin' After Midnight". The song went well and she exited the stage to thundering applause. The energy of the crowd inspired her and gave her courage. Glancing in her mother's direction, she saw she was involved in a conversation with a man wearing a bright orange suit and pink tie. Perhaps a wannabe music executive who liked the attention. Destynee took advantage of her mother's distraction and hurried off stage in the opposite direction and out of sight. She made a beeline for the nearest exit.

"That was really good." A young man holding drumsticks and wearing all black blocked her path.

"Thanks," she said and brushed past him.

"Hey. Don't be that way," he called out to her. "I just want to talk."

She ignored him and kept going. There were more nods and "great show" comments as she passed others waiting in the wings. She knew she could nail Patsy

Cline, even if her songs were not easy. Destynee had a low, sultry voice that hung on the notes and commanded attention. She had always been able to hold the audience in the palm of her hand from the first moment she opened her mouth. Her mother was right. It was a God-given talent that many others could only wish for. At that moment the praise did not mean anything. She just wanted to see her in-laws.

Craig, the stage manager, gave her a wide smile as she passed. "You killed it again this year, as usual."

"Thanks. You're going to make sure my mother has a ride back to the hotel, right?"

He shook his head and winked. "Got ya covered."

Deep down her thoughts were not really on her father-in-law, but on the husband and baby she felt as though she had abandoned. Travis had sided with her mother who always said her daughter shouldn't hide her talent. But the truth was Destynee never had aspirations to be famous until her mother convinced her that she could have a career as a singer. A notion that had been ingrained in her since the day she stood on the back porch and sang "God Bless America" to her family at their July Fourth backyard bar-b-que. Her destiny was decided then and there. Doris—that was her mother's real name—had vowed her baby would be a star one day. And Doris had never been able to break into the music scene as Julee Rae, so she turned her energies towards the next best thing. Her only daughter.

8
DESTYNEE

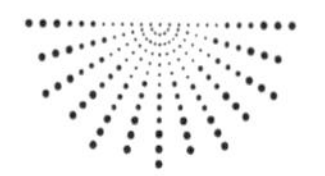

ARMED WITH A GIANT-SIZED DR. PEPPER AND pretzels she bought with the ten-dollar bill she happened to have stuffed in her pocket, Destynee set the cruise control a bit over the speed limit. She settled in, surfing through the radio stations until she found a Country Oldies station.

"Dang it!" she uttered aloud. Her cell phone was in her guitar case, which was still backstage at the arena. Craig would take care of her case until she got back, but she chided herself for forgetting the phone.

The good thing was her mother wouldn't be bothering her. The bad thing was she wouldn't be able to contact her husband Travis and let him know she was on her way. She would have to surprise everybody.

The drive went by fast. She sang along to the radio at the top of her lungs, and before no time she saw the glow of the city of Amarillo lighting the horizon. Fast food places were everywhere, only reminding her she hadn't eaten since that morning. Her mother kept a strict eye on her diet so that the costumes would always fit.

Julee Rae meant well, but that two-hour drive of alone time gave Destynee a relaxing reprieve. Exiting the interstate, she turned into the medical center and circled the parking lot three times until she found an open spot. She grabbed her wallet from the glove box, at least she had that. And at the last minute, remembered to remove her sparkly pink fringed shirt and tossed it into the back seat. Wearing a plain white T-shirt, she left her jeans tucked in her boots. The night air was a bit chilly. She shivered and walked faster.

The lobby was empty at this time of night, the smell of popcorn lingering in the air from the volunteer's cart. She doubted she would be allowed into the intensive care unit, but she could try. The lone receptionist looked bored and heavy-lidded, but smiled before answering her question, sending her to the sixth floor where coma patients were. The halls were eerie and quiet. Destynee wondered if she should be tip-toeing and then decided that would look ridiculous. Her boots echoed in the sterile hall.

She exited the elevator and followed the arrows and signs that read *ICU Waiting*. The room was empty, the television turned to the Weather Channel, and the smell of long overheated coffee hung heavy in the air from the silver pot in the corner. Taking a seat to think about what to do next, she hugged herself and rubbed her upper arms. Should she go to the nurses' station? But then she noticed the sign listing the visitation hours. Another hour and a half until visitors were allowed into the unit. She had all night.

~

Her eyes fluttered open from the warmth that suddenly encased her lap. She fought the heaviness of her lids. When Destynee looked up her husband Travis was holding his canvas jacket, the Rafter O brand embroidered in blue on the left front. At the sight of him she gasped. He was even more handsome than she remembered. The same crooked smile that always made her heart leap. How many days, weeks, had they been apart? It didn't matter because he was here now.

She stood immediately and walked into his arms, burying her face into his neck. He placed the jacket around her shoulders. It all came back to her. The warmth of his body. His smell. His touch. This was better than any fame or fortune.

"I missed you," he said.

She nodded, too overcome with emotion to speak.

Finally, she managed to ask, "How's Wyatt?"

"Growing."

They embraced without speaking for several moments more. He broke the searing touch and stepped away from her. "Where's your mother?"

"She doesn't know I'm here." Destynee straightened her shoulders and raised her chin in defiance.

Surprise crossed his face and then he smiled. "Thanks for coming."

He leaned forward to pick up the coffee cup that he had set down on an empty chair.

"Smells good."

"We have a while to wait until we can go in to see Dad. Let's go to the cafeteria and I'll buy you some fresh coffee."

"Do they have food?"

He laughed. "Your mother has you dieting again?"

She nodded. He took her hand and led her out of the waiting room to the elevator. They stepped in, coming together the minute the doors shut. Travis pressed her against the wall, kissing her until they were both breathless. He stepped back and gazed into her eyes. The kiss left her weak and wanting. There were no words to describe how happy she was at seeing her husband. A ding signaled the opening of the elevator, but her skin tingled long after the moment.

DESTYNEE ATE a ham sandwich from the vending machine and sipped hot coffee. Nothing had ever tasted so good in her life. While she chewed Travis talked. He told her about the horse wreck, the doctor's report, everything that had happened on the ranch since she left, and then he started talking about their son.

Despite the ache in her heart, she couldn't help but laugh. The boy certainly had personality plus.

"It's time. Come in with me to see my dad."

They cleared their table before heading back to the elevator. Without stopping at the waiting room again, he led her through double doors that read *No Admittance*. They walked through and stopped at the nurses' station. The male nurse smiled. "You can go on in. But just for ten minutes."

"Thank you."

Whatever Travis had said about his father's condition did not prepare her for what she saw. He must have lost at least fifteen pounds since she'd seen him last. His hair was completely white and cut close to his head, but he seemed to be at peace. Resting soundly. He didn't appear to be the same man without his cowboy hat and starched pearl snap shirt.

Travis gripped her hand tight as he stared at the man in the bed. "He doesn't seem to be in any pain."

"No, he doesn't." She held her breath and fought to maintain composure. She didn't want to cry now.

They stood there, side by side, Travis frozen still but never letting go of her hand.

The nurse appeared and reminded them that time was up. Without a word, Travis led his wife past the curtained cubicles towards the exit and back through the double doors. In the hall he turned to her.

"Destynee, stay with me. Please."

"Okay." He smiled at her answer and she smiled back. Of course she would stay. How could she leave her husband at a time like this?

Going back to the waiting room, they sat down on a vinyl sofa, arm in arm, and Destynee laid her head on his shoulder. Silent and still they waited.

EARLY THE NEXT MORNING, before dawn, Destynee and Travis ate breakfast in the hospital cafeteria. Still dark outside, the cafeteria was buzzing with medical personnel as some ended their shifts and others were just getting to work. Despite the worry, they couldn't take their eyes off each other.

"Will your mom be here this morning?" She didn't ask the question that was really on her mind. Was anyone bringing Wyatt to the hospital to see her?

"Yes. Everyone will be here at some point today. How long can you stay?"

"At least until noon, and then I had better head back." No matter what kind of punishment her mother could think of, it was worth it to see Travis, hold his hand.

"Tell me about the tour. How's it going?"

She snorted. "I wouldn't really call it a tour. It's my mother volunteering me for every county fair, chili cook-off, and church social she can find. I'm not so sure it's helping my career at all." A lump formed in her throat and she forced herself to swallow the tears. "I miss you."

"We miss you, too, but you are so talented. I promised you that I would never hold you back, if this is what you want."

"I don't know what I want." Tears pricked the back of her eyes.

"If you'll always wonder, then you have to keep going. Wyatt and I are behind you one hundred percent. In fact, we should probably come see you perform sometime. I just don't know your schedule."

"I know you support me, Travis. That means a lot." She said the words aloud, but deep inside she wanted to hear him beg her to come home. "I don't know my schedule until Mother gives it to me. She signs contracts right and left, she's always on the phone. I guess I'm lucky that she works so hard for me. I'll try to text you a few days ahead of time if I'm ever back in this area."

"I would like that. I don't think Wyatt has seen you sing on a real stage, except for church."

"Tell me more about him."

"He's great. I'll ask Mom to bring him."

"Okay." The response was weak and she wished she hadn't said anything. He looked at her in surprise. How could she tell him that seeing her son, smelling him and holding him would be the worst torture she could ever think of? How in the world will she ever be able to uphold the promises her mother had made to all the venues on her list? But mostly she struggled with the reason why anyone in their right mind would leave their precious child so they could sing for a crowd of strangers.

9
DESTYNEE

22 DAYS UNTIL CHRISTMAS

DESTYNEE HAD BOTH ARMS WRAPPED AROUND Travis's arm with her head leaned on his shoulder. They sat next to each other on the small couch in the ICU waiting room. She focused on his soft snores as he dozed and the sensation of having him close. How was it possible that she had almost forgotten the close bond they shared? She had missed him more than she realized.

Before she thought twice about it, she leaned closer. "Good morning." That grin again and her heart skipped. She pressed her lips to his. Soft and warm, the kiss tasted salty from the bag of chips they had shared several hours before. They didn't talk much, they never had to. Just being together was enough. Destynee wondered if her husband was praying for his father. Her thoughts were certainly filled with worry about her father-in-law, but they were focused more so on her son.

"Have y'all both been here all night?" Angie Olsen

stood in front of them, hands on her hips, looking all fresh and polished.

"Yeah," was all her brother mumbled as he blinked and ran his hand through his hair.

Destynee stood and hugged her sister-in-law. "Thanks for calling me, Angie."

"Of course. You're family. I'm so glad you're here." She looked over her shoulder. "Mom probably went the other way and wrangled a way into Dad's room. Thanks for staying all night, Travis. Mom got a good rest. I picked her up early this morning. She was on pins and needles to get back here."

"What about Wyatt?" Travis asked. "I left a message on her phone to bring him."

"I got it. I'm handling Mom's phone right now. The nanny will bring him."

In unison Destynee and Travis blurted out, "What nanny?"

Angie's eyes rolled upwards. "Travis, don't you remember? Mom said she mentioned it to you last week, even before this happened with Dad. She said she needed some help since she has a lot of commitments so she asked that girl from church, Kaylee. You said okay."

"I did?" He glanced at his wife.

"How old is this girl? Does she have a driver's license? How long has she been taking care of Wyatt? Travis, why didn't you talk to me about this?" Destynee was trying to get control of herself, but worry crept into her mind along with guilt. She should be the one at home with him.

"I'm sorry, Destynee. I guess a lot of things were happening at once. And sometimes it's hard to reach you."

She glared at him, too angry to speak.

"They'll be here later. Why don't you two go get coffee? You look like you could use some."

Travis pulled Destynee to her feet and they walked to the elevators. While they waited for the doors to open, she pulled her hand from his. He yawned and rubbed his face. She fumed in silence.

The cafeteria was still busy. Travis got in the food line and held out a tray. She shook her head. "Just coffee for me."

He shrugged. They found a table and Travis dug into his second breakfast that morning. He had smothered everything in gravy so she couldn't tell what all he had piled on the plate.

Destynee watched him eat until she felt like she'd explode or burst into tears. Either one, her emotions were in turmoil. She had never considered someone other than her husband or Grace taking care of Wyatt. She was obligated to finish out the December shows and then she could be home with Wyatt. Her absence was temporary. The need for a nanny had never crossed her mind.

Finally, she had to break the silence. "We need to talk."

He mumbled, still chewing.

"Why didn't you tell me that you might hire a nanny? I can't believe you don't keep me informed about our son."

He looked at her with a blank face and shrugged his shoulders. "She's just a babysitter. I honestly don't remember Mom mentioning her. With Dad in the hospital, we obviously need someone to watch Wyatt so my mother can be here. We're doing the best we can."

"Who is she?"

Without answering, Travis continued to eat. With the

last half of a biscuit, he cleaned up the last bit of gravy, wiped his mouth with a napkin, and drained his coffee cup.

"We should be a team. Any decision relating to Wyatt should be made together. I need to be kept in the loop, Travis. I'm his mother. I can't believe you've shut me out like this."

Anger glinted in Travis's eyes. "There is no loop, Destynee. It's just me and Wyatt. And thank goodness I have family close to help us."

His comment cut deep, whether he meant it to or not. The coffee suddenly turned over in her stomach. She stifled a sob but she couldn't stop the sudden tears that filled her eyes.

Regret showed on Travis's face. "I'm sorry. That was a low blow."

"You're right. I'm not here." Destynee swallowed the lump in her throat. "I'll meet you back upstairs."

She stood and left the cafeteria, escaping into the nearest restroom. She had no idea what time it was, but she would have to be leaving soon. A complete sense of hopelessness washed over her as she stared at her reflection in the mirror. A washed-up rodeo queen who had lost her crown and now her family. Her career was going nowhere and she was a lousy mother. For a girl with so much potential, she was spiraling downward into being nothing.

Splashing cold water on her face made her feel a bit better. She wet a paper towel to wash the back of her neck. The cold felt good. She had to pull herself together. It wouldn't do to burst out crying the minute she saw her son again.

Destynee wandered back to the ICU waiting area where Travis was sitting with his sister.

"Wyatt should be here any minute." Angie gave Destynee a look of excitement and then turned to look down the hall. "Here they come now."

Destynee watched a girl, maybe her age, or a little younger. Sunglasses, messy bun on the top of her head, with tendrils of black curls spiraling down her back. Destynee stared at the long red painted nails and hoped she wouldn't stab her baby. Toting a giggling Wyatt on one hip, his diaper bag slung over her opposite shoulder. Destynee's knees almost buckled at the sight of her son.

"Hey guys! We finally made it. My little man here wanted more Fruit Loops. I didn't think he'd ever get full."

Wyatt had grown so much in the past few months, she hardly recognized him. She could see Travis in his face, and parts of herself as well. The endearing grin was still there, he had always been a happy baby, but when Wyatt's eyes settled on her they passed over and locked onto his father. He giggled and squirmed to get out of the hands that held him.

"Hey, Sweetheart. It's Mommy." Destynee walked closer and held out her arms. "May I have my son, please?"

10
DESTYNEE

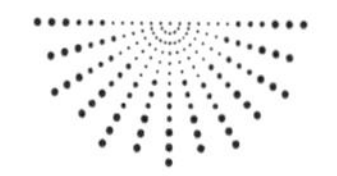

"OH, HELLO. YOU'RE HIS MAMA. YOU'RE Destynee. Sure, here ya go."

But Wyatt took one look at Destynee and fought to hold onto Kaylee.

"No! Kay Kay!"

His lower lip formed a pout and his eyes filled with unshed tears.

"Wyatt, come to Mama. Be a good boy." Destynee put her hand on his back but he kicked some more, burying his face in Kaylee's neck. And then Wyatt looked directly at her and shook his head no. Her heart was torn out at that very second and Destynee wondered if she would ever recover.

"Give him to me, Kaylee," Travis said.

But Wyatt couldn't be consoled now. He wriggled furiously and hollered, "Kay Kay! Hold me."

"What's going on? I can hear you from way down the hall." Nathan walked into the waiting room and took Wyatt from Kaylee. "Settle down now. It can't be that bad."

Destynee felt even more defeated watching Nathan with her son. Wyatt seemed to quiet immediately and lay his head on his uncle's shoulder while staring at her with wide, cautious eyes. Even Travis looked dejected. What a pair they made—they wouldn't be winning any awards for the perfect parenting team.

The nanny quietly spoke. "I'm so sorry. Maybe I shouldn't have given him that sugary cereal this morning."

"It's not your fault, Kaylee." Angie patted the girl on her shoulder.

Grace Olsen suddenly came through one of the doors. "What in the world? I can hear y'all in Skip's room. Oh, hey, Destynee." She gave her daughter-in-law a little hug.

"I'm sorry, Grace. Wyatt is putting up a fuss. He doesn't want to come to me. It's like he doesn't know who I am." Destynee's eyes filled with tears.

"Come here, Wyatt. Come to Meme." She held her arms out to the boy who grunted a little and half-turned back to Nathan, but then smiled at his grandmother. "He loves his uncle. That's a good boy," she said. "Now you're making your mama sad. Let her hold you. She came all this way."

Destynee smiled at Wyatt and turned her head playfully to one side to try and entice him. She held out her hands to take him from Grace. But then the kicking and screaming started all over again, as if she had done something horrible to him.

An ICU nurse poked her head into the designated ICU waiting room. "You are going to have to quiet that child. Take him to the other waiting room in the main lobby area on the first floor. There's a children's play area. You can't stay here."

"We're sorry," said Angie.

"Of course he knows who you are," Grace told Destynee as she patted Wyatt. "You've been gone awhile. This is his way of acting out and letting you know he's mad that you've been gone. He sees me, and now Kaylee, every day. Don't be upset. Give him a kiss."

Destynee leaned closer and kissed his soft cheek, which she was surprised he had allowed. She could feel the tears on her face, but couldn't stop them. She looked at Travis. "I need to get going anyway. It's almost noon."

"Destynee, wait. Stay awhile. Wyatt'll come around. He just needs to get used to you again."

To Grace she said, "I'm sorry. I'll be praying for Skip. Please keep me posted. I'll try to come again soon." To the whole group she said, "I'm sorry. I've got to go." She turned back to Wyatt and said, "I love you, baby."

"Let me walk you to your car." Travis followed her into the hall and slung an arm around her shoulder.

"I'm fine. I don't need you to walk me to my car. I can handle it." She shrugged his arm off and then regretted it after she saw the pained look on his face.

"And that's part of the problem. You don't need me," he murmured. "Go ahead. I'm not going to be the one to stop you, but text me when you get there."

As she waited at the elevator, she looked back to see her husband still standing in the same spot. Frozen still, in the middle of the hallway with a look of utter sadness covering his handsome face. Her heart broke again, if that were even possible. She wanted to run back into his arms and start the day over, but the elevators opened and she stepped inside without another glance in his direction.

Running to her car she hopped in and floored it out of the parking lot. Glancing in the rearview mirror through a flood of tears, she thought about Travis standing solid like a beacon in a rough sea watching her speed out of his life once again. How long could they keep this up? She felt her little family was tearing apart at the seams. And she had no idea what to do about it.

Wiping her face with the back of her hand, she switched her mind to robot mode. The clock told her she'd be back in a couple of hours. Hopefully in time for the chili cook off event. Sooner if she drove faster.

Focused on driving, she tried not to think about her husband and son and what had happened at the hospital. She couldn't afford to think about it. Just do your job. But who has a chili cook-off in the middle of December anyway? Wasn't that a fall event? And how did her mother keep finding obscure events in these little towns? It didn't make sense to her how this endless schedule was propelling her career anyway. She wiped tears from her face with a napkin from the console. It was time she had a heart-to-heart talk with Julee Rae.

It had been a bit of a relief to not have her cell phone at the hospital. She was sure her mother would have been calling her non-stop. And now on this drive she was sure Travis would be trying to call her to make sure she made it back safely. Maybe the world would be a better place if people went back to old-fashioned ways and waited until they saw people to talk to them. None of this "tied to the hip" business, at one another's beck and call twenty-four hours a day. Although she had to admit they came in handy in times of emergency. Like if something happened to Wyatt. Darn, why did her mind go there? Turn it off, she told herself. Just drive. Be a zombie. Don't think of him. Don't think about mothering. It just wasn't meant to be her life now. And she couldn't do a gosh darn thing about it. Just drive.

Her car screeched to a stop in the gravel parking lot of the motel. She tapped on the door to their room.

The door flung open and a furious woman stared back at her. "Where in the world have you been? Gone all night. This is the thanks I get? After all the sacrifices I make for you." She sniffed, her expression frustrated.

"I told you I had to go to the hospital, Mother." She had never noticed how much the world revolved around Julee Rae, and how she could churn up fake tears on a dime.

"*Hmpff*. Well, how's Skip anyway?"

At least she had the courtesy to ask. "Still in a coma. They're watching him closely."

"Was everyone there?"

"Yes."

"Travis?"

"Yes."

"Well?"

"Well, what? I really don't want to talk about it. I'm here now. How much time do we have?"

Destynee tried to go inside but her mother continued to block the doorway.

"A couple hours till your soundcheck and then it's show time."

"Fine. I need to get my cell phone out of my guitar case."

"You no longer have access to a cell phone." The words hung in the awkward silence that stretched between them. Destynee was too stunned to reply.

"You don't need to be bothered by any calls right now. I need you to keep your head on straight. You've got work to do. I've been busy while you've been off doing your own thing." Julee Rae pursed her lips. "I made some new contacts that might be very good for your career. I'll tell ya about them later."

Destynee stared at her mother in disbelief, and then decided to save this argument about her phone for another time. She shouldn't be surprised that there would be consequences. But this discussion wasn't over and it didn't go unnoticed that Julee Rae had failed to mention her own grandson or even ask how he was doing.

She met her mother's gaze. "Fine. What am I wearing?"

11
DESTYNEE

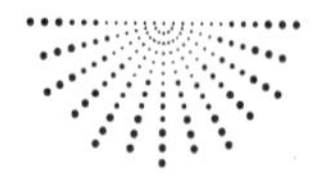

THE ANNUAL CHRISTMAS CRAFT SHOW AND chili cook-off was held at the Brown County Fairgrounds. Destynee had played the event several years ago, but her mother had gotten crosswise with the organizer that year and they weren't invited back. They must have had a change of personnel for her mother to book them again, although she didn't ask. It was better not knowing the details. Her job was to sing. She liked it like that.

Julee Rae steered the car into a grassy field that served as the parking lot. She wove in between cars and pickup trucks with livestock trailers haphazardly parked in crooked rows.

"Good grief. You'd think these rednecks could park their cars in a straight line."

Everything and everybody annoyed Julee Rae. Destynee tried to roll with the flow, but her mother acted horribly if things didn't go exactly how she thought they should. One of the reasons her mother was always unhappy. It made for an exhausting day. When the car came to a stop, Destynee got out quickly and retrieved her guitar case from the backseat. Without another word, she turned and walked towards the oversized Quonset barn to find a place behind the stage where she could stay out of sight until time for her to sing. She had been mulling over the song list all day.

Still miffed about the cell phone situation, she leaned towards singing an original song. There wasn't anything much worse that her mother could do to her. She had written it several years ago about a girl and her love for the rodeo. Destynee was never allowed to do anything on her horses but look pretty, carry a flag into the arena, and stay in the saddle while doing it. But she had always wanted to ride barrels. To fly with the wind, the only competition being the clock. She admired the girls who had the guts to do that. And most of them were true cowgirls. Not only could they ride extremely well, but they could rope and train their horses, too. She hummed the tune as she walked.

Without looking behind to see if her mother was following, Destynee walked inside. The barn was bursting with people. Vendor booths were organized in neat rows with everything from homemade jams to detailed leather work for sale. She stopped at a table display of jewelry. Pathetic really that a married woman with a toddler had no wallet because her mother did not allow it. A purse ruined the image.

"Are you singing for us?" A woman asked.

"Yes, I am." Destynee smiled at her. "Any special requests?"

She laughed. "Oh, my. I have so many favorites, I'd never be able to decide."

Destynee looked through a rack of necklaces with varying colors of stones. She'd never owned anything so pretty.

"Do you like those? I made them. Hang on, I have something you need." The lady pulled a wooden box out from under the counter. Inside were various sections, each with a necklace. "See one you like?"

"They are all beautiful."

"Here. Try this one." The woman pulled out a short necklace with red stones. "These are red coral." She fastened it around Destynee's neck. It lay just below her throat and matched her dress perfectly. Her mother had allowed her to skip the sequins since the venue was a barn.

"I don't have any money with me." She unfastened it, but the woman stopped her.

"Keep it. When you're on stage you can tell them to stop by Sierra's Jewels."

"All right. I can do that, but I really don't want to take your necklace."

"I insist. You look beautiful wearing it."

Destynee gave the woman a hug. "I love it. Thank you."

She made her way to the stage area, if you could call it that. Tucked in the very back corner behind a semi-circle of hay bales stood a microphone. There were several people standing or sitting on the hay bales. One held a fiddle. A group of kids, she would guess sister and her two brothers because they were dressed the same, all smiled as she walked closer.

A woman with a clipboard suddenly appeared at her side. "Name."

"Destynee."

"What's your talent?"

"I'm singing."

"Oh, you're the headliner." Surprise showed in her eyes. "You go on last. Are you that good?"

An odd question, but this was news to her as well. "I will do my best."

She perched on the very last hay bale and scanned the crowd. The noise was deafening in the tin building. It was perfect. She pulled her guitar out of the case, strummed and softly sang several songs. And then built the courage up to sing her own song. Playing a few chords, she ran the words over in her mind to remember them.

Where did you come from, my beautiful son?
Sent from heaven like an angel to earth.
Daddy's proudest legacy. Mama's whole heart.
We'll always love you; don't you ever doubt.
Thanking God for His gift of you, binding us
together forever.
Daddy's proudest legacy. Mama's whole heart.

"I think you should start with Patsy Cline."

Destynee jumped at the sound of her mother's voice. Her heart pounded. She wasn't usually this nervous.

"There are a lot of old people here. They'll like that." Julee Rae looked over the crowd and frowned. "I'm not sure they even listen to today's country music."

"Of course, they do," Destynee said. Her mother wandered away, thank goodness.

A group of young kids arrived, bursting with nervous energy and guitars, dressed in black. They even had a trap set and were raring to go.

"We have a dressing room for you." The young woman with the clipboard appeared again. "Come this way."

Destynee followed her to the other side of the barn where an office had been constructed. They passed through a small room with barely enough room for a desk, file cabinets, and printer. The woman stopped and opened a door.

"This is yours."

Destynee stepped into an even smaller room. A closet really. File boxes were stacked to one side of the room from floor to ceiling. Oversized candy canes were piled in one corner. In the middle was an easy chair and a table with bottles of water, a bowl of fruit, and peanut butter crackers. She'd never had her own dressing room before. It wasn't fancy but she liked it.

"Public restrooms are back through the way we came in and to your right. If you need anything, come find me."

"Thank you."

Closing the door, she sank into the chair. Alone. She sighed. Her mother was going to have heart failure if she couldn't freshen up the makeup and fiddle with her hair for at least an hour. Maybe the vendor booths would keep Julee Rae occupied and distracted.

If she had her phone, she'd call Travis. She whispered a prayer for Skip, prayed for strength for her husband, and a watchful eye over her son. She wished that Travis was more proficient with the camera on his phone so he could text her pictures of Wyatt. A sadness suddenly washed over her, so deep and so hopeless, she couldn't think and she lost her breath. She strummed her guitar until she felt better, focusing on her music instead of her son's toddler face.

By the time someone knocked on the door, she still couldn't shake the sadness but she covered her face with the widest smile ever and walked into the barn. The young drummer was giving it his all.

"And now we have a real treat for you folks. Straight from Dixon, Texas. Please welcome Destynee!"

Maybe three people clapped, but most everyone kept shopping and talking. She stepped on stage, which was the space behind the hay bales and in front of the drum set. Nodding her appreciation to the kid, but instead of stopping he finished an amazing drum solo. She appreciated his talent but wanted to get on with things.

With that final cymbal crash still ringing in her ears, she turned to see about a dozen people standing on the other side of the hay bales.

"I'd like to start with one of my own original songs."

12
TRAVIS

21 DAYS UNTIL CHRISTMAS

TRAVIS SAT MOTIONLESS IN THE ICU WAITING room while the rest of his family took turns visiting his father. Kaylee had finally left with Wyatt. There wasn't anything any of them could do to settle him down. While Grace explained that's how toddlers are, Travis was convinced that seeing his mother had upset Wyatt as much as it had Destynee. Of course, the toddler remembered her. Travis agreed with his mother. Wyatt was upset that she's been gone and the only way he knew how to communicate was to cry and carry on.

Travis had become so wrapped up in his own pity party, he forgot how her absence might affect Wyatt. His son was suffering, too. And what he really wanted to know was, if this whole plan of going on the road for her singing career was Destynee's wish or Julee Rae's.

He closed his eyes and focused on her face, trying to remember the feel of her in his arms. It had only been a few hours ago since she left, but in the light of day the night before seemed like a dream. Still, when he took a deep breath, her scent still lingered on his jacket, overpowering the smell of day-old coffee and hospital disinfectant.

Seeing her again only strengthened his doubts about having encouraged her to leave. What was he thinking? Was her career more important at this stage in Wyatt's life? He had never voiced his opinion openly before, but he questioned the motives of his mother-in-law. He wasn't so sure that she had Destynee's best interests at heart.

Other thoughts weighed him down, too. Instead of dozing, the events of the accident played over and over in his mind. Maybe he could have done something. His father tossed the loop, he jerked it taut, and that other calf came out of nowhere. If only, if only, if only. He'd lose his mind rehashing everything. He really needed Destynee beside him. She was his sounding board and sense of reason. He dialed her number. No answer. She was supposed to text when she got to the motel. He dialed her number again but did not leave a message when it went straight to voicemail.

Angie suddenly appeared from around the corner, her eyes wide and brimming with unshed tears. "He's awake!"

Travis stared at his sister for a minute, trying to make sense of what she had just said. Before he could respond, she spun around and disappeared. His first instinct was to call Destynee, but he would try again later. He hurried after his sister, going through the double doors into the ICU unit ignoring the visitation hours. In the cubicle, his mom and dad were staring at each other. Grace gripped Skip's hand so tight, her knuckles were turning white. Angie stood on the other side of his bed, a big smile on her face and tears running down her cheeks.

He stopped at the foot of the bed, both hands resting on the footboard. "Dad?" Travis leaned closer. Skip slowly turned his head to look at his youngest son.

When Travis met his father's eyes, his knees grew weak and he thought he might pass out right then from relief. His dad's eyes were bright and clear, no pain reflected in his stare. Although they may be giving him pain killers. The question was, is everything in working order?

"Good to see you awake," Travis said.

"We need to call your brother and sisters," Grace said. "Travis, can you do that? But before you leave, let's give thanks."

They bowed their heads, closed their eyes.

"Heavenly Father, we give thanks that Skip is still with us. Give him strength and healing. Thank you for the capable people who work at this medical center and who are caring for him. We ask that you bless them in their lives and in their work. Amen."

Travis murmured "Amen," and walked over to his mother to give her a kiss on the cheek, rested his hand for a minute over both of his parents' clasped hands, and then returned back into the main hall to make the phone calls. First, he did a group text to Nathan, Janie, and Libbie, and then he punched Destynee's number. It rang and switched to voicemail, so he left a message. "Dad's awake. Call me when you can." And just before ending the call, added, "I love you."

A text came back immediately from Nathan. "Wyatt is doing fine. Indya will stay here with both boys. I'm headed your way."

Travis realized how lucky he was to have such a

supportive family to help with his son. God knows, he had done a terrible job of it so far. He hoped Destynee realized it, too. None of the Olsens ever spoke bad about her or about her decision to pursue a musical career. Travis couldn't explain it, but he just knew that if their marriage was going to stand the test of time, it had to be Destynee who came back on her own. She was the one who had to choose. He had made his choice the very first time he had looked into her blue eyes.

A text came back from Janie. *On my way.*

Of course, still nothing from his sister Libbie who was at Baylor. She had willingly stepped into the next phase of her life and never looked back. He couldn't imagine a life anywhere but where he was. If Destynee decided otherwise, well, he'd cross that bridge when he came to it.

He hurried back to his father's room and gave his mother an update.

"The doctor will be here sometime between five and six to talk with us," she said.

All the Olsen siblings were en route and would be together when the doctor made his rounds that evening. Travis was anxious to hear the prognosis.

SKIP OLSEN'S wife and kids gathered around his hospital bed. He had been moved out of the Intensive Care Unit to a regular room on the tenth floor. Travis watched his father gaze at each precious member in turn, a contemplative expression on his face. He was about to speak. Travis had seen that look before.

He wished Destynee could be here, too. He had called her several times, left numerous text messages, but no word back. No telling what Julee Rae had roped her into, but he had hoped she might have this Sunday afternoon off so they could talk. If he couldn't have her by his side, he wanted to at least hear her voice again.

Skip cleared his throat. "I am sure thankful to the good Lord to see your faces again."

Travis noticed the tears streaming down his mother's face, but she didn't speak. None of them could speak as they waited on Skip to say what he needed to say. He pointed to the water. Grace held the cup and straw for him.

"I don't know how long they'll keep me here, and no matter, as long as the work on the Rafter O continues. Angie. You know as much as anybody. You ramrod this thing and keep it moving along. If you have questions, call me anytime. Your mother can help with the bookkeeping. Janie can keep the equipment in working order. Travis. You help your sisters. Whatever they need. I want you to make yourself available."

Travis nodded and met his father's eyes. He could do that, but he may have to get a part-time job at the feed store in order to afford the babysitter in case his mother couldn't watch Wyatt. Guilt washed over him as he recognized the resentment towards his wife growing. "Of course, we'll do whatever needs to be done, Dad." Angie placed a hand on his shoulder. "You just rest and get better."

"I'm here, too," Janie, the oldest daughter, said. "Whatever you need. Just let me know, and my husband can help too. You know Mack and I are here for you and Mom."

"I love every one of ya," Skip said, his eyes brimming with tears. "I just have one other request."

"Sure, Dad."

"Anything," Nathan said.

"You name it," said Travis. He looked from one face to the other. They were stronger together and their family would get through this crisis.

"Can someone tell me exactly what happened in the pen because the last thing I remember is seeing the loop of my rope sail through the air."

Nervous laughter filled the room and broke the seriousness of the situation as Travis and Nathan tried to relay the story. Skip was becoming a legend in his own right.

13
TRAVIS

TRAVIS WATCHED HIS PRECIOUS BOY SLEEP IN the crib Grace had bought for them. The longer he sat there, the madder he got. Seeing his wife again raised so many doubts and questions. How could the mother of this precious child walk away without a word? He had tried to call her many times, but she wasn't answering his calls. And then he chided himself for his selfish thoughts. She was following her dream.

Probably busy with her singing gigs. Was she even thinking about him? About Wyatt? Did her mother have her running ragged from one town to the next that she couldn't even spare one minute and give him a call? Was she upset with him? Why?

He wasn't sure how long they could survive this living situation. This wasn't the way he had imagined married life to be—living together, in one household, mother and father with their child. He had loved Destynee for a long time now, and if truth be known, they had wanted to get pregnant even before they were married. He knew it wasn't the Christian thing to do, but her mother had such a stranglehold on the girl and she had forbidden them from marrying. Said they were too young. Said Destynee had to think of her singing career first and foremost. That she'd only have this opportunity once in her life.

They both knew they were treading in dangerous waters. He should have been stronger and kept his distance. He should have stood up to her mother and convinced her of their desire to marry. But Destynee had begged him to not make waves. At the same time, neither of them could stay away from each other, no matter how hard they had tried. Later they both knew they should have listened and followed their Christian upbringing. Travis remembered once in church the pastor talking about following the Bible almost like it was an instruction manual for life. "In the long run," the pastor had said, "it makes your life easier if you follow the rules. God had a good reason, a loving reason, for giving them to us. He was trying to protect us from the evil pitfalls of this world."

Easier said than done, Travis thought. Yes, they realized they had been rebellious and done what they had wanted to do. But neither of them ever regretted Wyatt's birth. He was their child and it was meant for all of them to be together.

So, what was he supposed to do? His head was throbbing. He just wanted it all to go away. He wanted peace. Not all this indecision.

Wyatt suddenly opened his eyes, and in the pool of the night-light Travis could see tears welling up in his eyes.

"Mama," he said.

Travis had to laugh despite the seriousness of the

situation. Of course, Wyatt remembered his mama. That little stinker.

"Mama's not here, but I am." He picked him up out of the crib and sat down in the rocking chair. They rocked for several minutes while Travis sang an old cowboy song, "My Rifle, My Pony and Me." A soothing ballad about a cowboy at the end of a long workday was one of Travis's favorites.

Wyatt drifted off to sleep again, so Travis slowly stood and gently laid him into the crib. The minute his little back hit the mattress, his eyes snapped open and he let out a blood curdling scream.

"Okay, okay," said Travis. He picked him up again.

They were both wide awake now. Poor little guy had been disrupted a lot these last few days. Grace had mentioned several times that kids do better with a set schedule. Easy enough to offer advice, but impossible for a single parent to execute sometimes.

"How about a snack?"

Travis padded to the kitchen with Wyatt balanced on one hip. He clicked on the kitchen light and a slight grin spread over his son's face. Yep. Wide awake now.

"Apple? Banana? Fish crackers?" Travis's suggestions got no response from Wyatt, only a big wide grin as he placed him in the highchair. "How about a little of everything?"

He peeled and sliced an apple. Cut a banana into chunks, piling a few pieces of each on the tray along with a pile of cheddar cheese toddler snacks. Wyatt dug in. Travis had to find his phone and take a few pictures. Their little guy was so darn cute, happily eating snacks at midnight.

After he snapped a few pics, he sent them to

Destynee with the text, "Call me when you see this. No matter what time."

He thought of his brother Nathan. So take-charge when their father was out cold on the ground after the accident. Take-charge in the hospital when Wyatt was pitching a fit. Nathan had grown into a strong, decisive man in the last few years. Travis remembered Nathan's own indecisiveness before he married Indya when he was searching for his life's path. When he couldn't stand up to their father who almost demanded that Nathan take over the ranch according to Olsen tradition, oldest son and all that. But Nathan had struggled. He wanted to be an artist, not a rancher. So opposite to his dad's plans. It had to come to a breaking point for Nathan to voice his own desires, to follow his own heart, not his father's dreams. There was some heartache, some anger, even feelings of abandonment when Nathan left home and moved to Santa Fe for a time.

But look at him now. He met and married Indya. They had a son. Both working on their love of art and even opened a gallery in Amarillo. Still close enough to the family, but far enough away to have their own space. It appeared they had a happy life now. Would that ever happen for him, Destynee, and Wyatt?

What would it take? Should he "be a man" and put his foot down? Demand Destynee come home and be a wife and mother? Tell her mother to back off, take a hike?

He dropped his face into his hands. Dear God, help us. I don't know what to do. What about her singing? How can I take that away from her? Wouldn't she hate me later? And it's a gift from You.

So tired. And no answers. He just wanted to sleep and forget it all.

He remembered the bottle of liquor he had left on the side table next to the couch. Should he? Just one drink.

But he knew he had to work at the ranch in the morning. Angie had mentioned it at the hospital in very serious tones. Travis could tell she wanted to say more but not in front of everyone. Her face even got red. Was she upset with him? Didn't she have Nathan to help? Or was he busy with his own family? And Colton, her boyfriend? Travis didn't even know if they were still together. Maybe not. Why was Angie bugging him? Every so often she pulled out that older sister card. Couldn't she mind her own business and just leave him alone?

Although, actually, he was sick and tired of being alone. Destynee had left him to handle Wyatt and everything about their life on his own. Every day, every night he was alone. He missed her so much. The smell of her hair, the softness of her body. He loved being next to her. Now he felt like half a man.

Maybe it would be good if Angie, or someone, gave him a good kick in the pants to get him going again. He needed to straighten out his own life and give his son the best childhood possible.

He'd have to get Wyatt ready for the new babysitter who would pick him up at the Rafter O. What was her name? Oh yeah, Kaylee. She seemed to be another obstacle between him and Destynee. Why? She was just a babysitter. Would he ever understand women?

Wyatt began to nod off in his highchair, so Travis cleaned his hands and mouth and put him back to bed. He was sound asleep within seconds of his head touching the pillow. A full belly sure made sleeping easier.

Wandering out to the back porch of the small, ramshackle house Travis looked up to the stars. It wasn't as beautiful and wide open or as dark as being on the Rafter O, but at least he could breathe a bit better. Always he had his ears attuned for any sound from Wyatt's room.

He pulled out his phone and tried Destynee again. No answer. He hadn't really expected her to pick up. But he left another message.

Where was she? He wished she could have stayed longer, maybe spent at least one night. Why didn't she want to be with him? With Wyatt. At home.

Travis hit the shower, let the hot water take the tension from the past few days and seep out of his shoulders. He collapsed on the bed, closed his eyes, and just before he drifted to sleep, he again remembered that unopened bottle still waiting on the side table in the living room. He never had time to take a drink.

His son had saved him.

14
TRAVIS

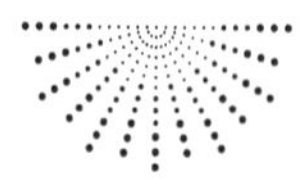

20 DAYS UNTIL CHRISTMAS

THE NEXT MORNING, HE WOKE UP ON THE couch, not sure when in the night he made the switch. It had become his routine since Destynee left. Travis just didn't feel comfortable in their bed without her. It was too empty. Most nights he fell asleep in the rocker in Wyatt's room after story time and then moved to the living room during the night. He only used the room he shared with his wife to get dressed.

Wyatt was already awake and babbling. That was one happy little boy. Most of the time.

Travis stumbled off the couch, rubbed his head and scruff of a short beard. Why bother shaving? He didn't have anywhere to be or anyone who cared what he did.

"Good morning, little man."

That wide grin that greeted him every morning made his heart swell. Wyatt was standing in his crib. Giggles galore flew out of his mouth. "Dada!" Then his pj-covered feet started the happy dance he did a lot. Tiny feet marching up and down. So excited to see his dad. He never imagined that he could love this kid so much. He would do anything for his son. The mornings were the toughest and only made him wish more that his wife could be here to watch him, too.

"Come on, big boy. Are ya wet?" Travis felt his son's bottom. Yes, of course he'd have to be changed. Travis tried to etch in his brain to remember to do some laundry tonight, at least Wyatt's pajamas. Pretty soon the boy would be sleeping in just a diaper if Travis didn't do some chores. Destynee used to take care of all that stuff. And sometimes his mother helped. But they could never rely on his mother-in-law, even when they moved in with her at Destynee's insistence. Come to think of it, had it really been his wife's idea?

Julee Rae had never changed one diaper, read a bedtime story, or even rocked her only grandchild to sleep. Her sole focus was Destynee and her singing career. It was very odd, the more Travis thought about it, and he'd had plenty of time to think after they left him alone in the house to go back on the road.

He had no choice but to pull his weight and take care of everything. He was Wyatt's father after all. A single dad it seemed. No matter the circumstances he found himself in, he didn't want to be a deadbeat dad. Or a drunk. But he couldn't seem to pull himself out of the funk that he had sunk into. This wasn't the life he had imagined, without Destynee by his side.

He picked Wyatt up, the boy's little arms stretched around Travis's neck. Placing the child on the changing table, Travis wiped his little body clean with a sanitized wipe as the baby kicked and squealed full of happiness on this new day.

"Come on, Wyatt. Settle down so's I can get your clothes on you. You're like a wiggling fish."

Surprisingly, a knock sounded at the door and he heard his sister's voice.

"Travis, you up? I need to talk to you."

He grabbed Wyatt and headed to open the door to find his sister standing on the front porch, hands on hips, and a determined look on her face. This couldn't be good.

"Angie. What're you doin' here? It's not even seven, is it?

"It might be early for you, but this detour is making me late to start chores on the ranch. I needed to talk to you before the day gets too far along."

"What about?"

"Helping me." He was surprised at the desperation in her voice. She walked closer and tickled Wyatt's tummy. "Good morning, sweet boy."

"You kinda mentioned that at the hospital. I was getting Wyatt and me ready to head that way soon."

"Might I remind you what Dad said, and I quote, 'make yourself available.'"

"I was there. I heard him." Travis didn't hide the deep frown that creased his forehead.

"Well, good. You know, Travis, you've been wallerin' a long time now over Destynee. It's time you quit that and got your stuff together. And trying to numb your pain with alcohol, that's over too. I hope you realize that'll get you nowhere."

"Why don't you just tell it like it is, Sis? Don't pull any punches."

"Brother of mine, you know our family speaks plainly. We're not going to coddle you or pretend we don't see what you're doing to yourself. The thing is you've got a son. You need to man up, take responsibility, and do what's right. Plus, with Dad recuperating and Nathan busy with his own family and business, I really need the help on the ranch."

She wasn't telling him anything he didn't know already. He turned his back to her and walked towards the kitchen. "You want coffee? I could use some and Wyatt needs his breakfast."

She followed them. "Sure, I'll take a cup. Here, let me hold that little rascal."

Wyatt let out a joyful squeal and kicked his legs when his father set him on the floor. He toddled over to Angie's legs and she bent down to pick him up and plant kisses on his chubby cheeks.

"Put him in the highchair and I'll get him some cereal and a banana."

"Hope you're not giving him that sugary stuff like he had the other day." She let out an exhale.

"He does like that a lot. Let's not mention the name. I'll give him Cheerios. He's good with those, too."

Once they got Wyatt settled, Travis poured two coffees.

Angie looked around the kitchen. "It sure is yellow in here. How old is that refrigerator? This doesn't look like you at all, Brother."

"My mother-in-law is not much of a homemaker. She's all about a musical career. First hers, and now her daughter's."

"And they left you to raise your son alone. I'm not sure if I agree with that." She turned to look at Wyatt with sad eyes. "He has two parents, ya know."

"You can't deny that my wife can sing."

Angie nodded in agreement. "She has one of the most

beautiful voices I've ever heard, but sometimes in life your priorities change."

"Speaking of life, what about your boyfriend Colton? Can't he help? I remember how upset he was the day of Dad's accident."

"Colton and I are not seeing each other. Yes, he's a family friend, but that's about all right now. You'd know that if you paid more attention to what was happening around the ranch."

"Angie, I think I've had my hands a little full with my own family. I can't keep up with your love life. And besides I really don't want to."

"Well, that's refreshing. You'd be one of the few people in this family that doesn't pay attention to my love life." They both shared a laugh, and then her expression got serious again. "I just want you to know there's a lot of work to be done and I want you to commit to helping me, one hundred percent. I think I speak for Dad too. I expect you to be there every morning bright and early. No hangover. No moping around."

"Is there anything else you can find to criticize me about? Please, continue." There was no denying he didn't deserve what she was dishing out.

She paused to take a sip of coffee. "The truth is I need you, Travis. And I'm very worried about Dad."

"What about Wyatt? He needs me, too."

"I realize that you've got Wyatt to think about. Who's gonna watch him while you're working? I know this is a burden for you, but surely, we can find a solution."

He stuttered a bit. "Uh, at the hospital Mom said that girl…uh, Kaylee I think is her name…she's looking for more work. She lives down the road with her parents."

"All right. That's good. I can add you to the ranch payroll so you can afford to pay her. No telling how much care Dad will need when he gets home, but one thing is for sure, Mom will want to do it all herself. And you know what that means, don't you?"

His brows pinched together. "What?"

"You gotta move back to the Rafter O."

"Why?"

"It'll just make it easier for everyone. Closer to Mom in case she needs you. Closer for Kaylee to watch Wyatt. Closer to your work in case I need you. That way, you'll never be late." She gave him a big sisterly smirk.

Sometimes he hated it when she was right. And bossy. But she had a point. He didn't like staying in this house anyway. Too much of Julee Rae's vibes. And sad, lonely thoughts without Destynee. Truth be told, he really hated living in town and now he had an excuse to leave.

His head pointed downward but his eyes flipped up towards her. "All right. I'll do it. Beats staying here. That's for sure. But there is one more thing."

She pressed her lips into a fine line and raised one eyebrow.

"I've been day working for several outfits, and I'd like to keep doing that. It makes a little cash and since they are starting to call me, I don't want to let anyone down."

"That's okay with me. I'm not sure we have enough to keep both of us busy during the winter anyway. Why don't you help me out today, pack your stuff tonight, and move everything to the ranch tomorrow? Talk to Mom. I'm sure she'll be happy to have you back in your old room."

"I'll leave Destynee a message too. So she'll know where we're gonna be staying."

"Why a message? Don't you two talk?"

He was quiet for what seemed like an eternity. Kind

of embarrassing to admit to his sister that he wasn't in touch with his wife much lately.

"She hasn't been returning any of my calls. I don't know why. Maybe she's too busy. Maybe she's upset with me."

"Over what?"

"I don't know. Maybe the way Wyatt wouldn't go to her at the hospital and preferred the babysitter. That caught her off guard, I think. Me too actually."

"But doesn't she want to check up on Wyatt, know how he's doing?"

"I don't know, Sis. It's complicated lately. Destynee's been really busy with all her singing obligations. Her mother keeps her schedule full. On the road to stardom and all that."

"How do you feel about it?"

"I want her to be happy and chase her dreams. But I also want her to be with us. I support her. This is for her to decide."

"She is very talented, I'll give you that, and she is lucky to have you as a husband. I guess it is complicated. Don't worry, Travis. It'll work out. But you've got to keep going with your own life. And Wyatt's. You can't just give up and stay on the couch."

"I know you're right. It's just really hard sometimes." He gulped his coffee and put the mug in the sink. "Right now, though, we're burnin' daylight. I'll get Wyatt's stuff and we'll head to the ranch in a few minutes."

"Okay. I'll take off. We can talk about what I need you to do when we get there." She gave her nephew a kiss on the head. He held out a chubby fist filled with squashed banana. She laughed. "No thank you."

Travis lifted Wyatt out of the highchair and walked his sister to the door.

Before she turned the knob, Travis called to her. "Angie?"

"Yeah?"

"Thanks."

She smiled and he grinned back. He had just thanked his sister for telling him what a loser he was. There was nothing like the love of family.

Before she got in the car, Angie waved and blew her nephew kisses which made him giggle.

Travis sighed as they both watched Angie back out of the driveway. "The sooner you learn to go along with whatever a woman tells you to do, the easier your life is gonna be, Wyatt."

The baby giggled.

15
TRAVIS

TRAVIS PULLED UP TO HIS PARENTS' HOUSE, looped the diaper bag over his shoulder, and balanced his son on the opposite hip. He was surprised to find the babysitter Kaylee already inside talking with his mother in the kitchen.

"Mornin', Travis. Is that my little cowboy Wyatt?" Grace proceeded to cover her grandson's face with kisses which produced giggles like a gurgling brook.

"Meme!" the boy squealed.

"Come over here. Let me hold you. Do you want a cookie?"

Wyatt held out his hand. "Pease."

"He wants peas?" Travis laughed.

"No, he's saying 'please'. We've been working on our manners. Please and thank you." She opened a bag of animal cookies and handed one to Wyatt.

"Really, Mother? Cookies this early?"

Grace ignored him. As she held the boy, the babysitter smiled while holding her coffee mug. "Hey,

Travis. I'm not sure if we formally met at the hospital. I'm Kaylee."

He nodded. "Hi, how are ya? I understand you might be available to watch Wyatt while I'm working."

"Yes, I could do that, if it's okay with you and your wife."

Travis looked at his mother, but thought of Destynee and remembered the hurtful look on her face. He felt uncomfortable. "Sure, that's fine. He seems to like you."

"He's a great kid. We have fun together."

Angie buzzed into the kitchen and grabbed a muffin from the counter. "Mom. Travis is moving back home." And then she was out the backdoor again.

Grace looked at her son in surprise. "You are?"

"Is it okay with you and Dad if Wyatt and I stay here a while?" And then he added, "It was Angie's idea. That way I'll be close if you or Dad needs anything, and easier for Kaylee to help with Wyatt."

Pathetic to hide behind your sister, but he had to admit he didn't want to seem that eager. Also, sad that a grown man with a wife and child actually liked the idea of moving back in with his parents.

"Of course it is, Son. We'd love to have you. Stay as long as you want."

"Well, if you ladies are okay, I'd better get out to the barn and see what Angie has for me to do." He leaned into Wyatt. "And you be a good boy, okay?" He pointed his finger at his son, then gave him a kiss on the cheek.

"Travis, I think we have some boxes for your move, if you need them. Don't forget to ask me for them before you leave tonight."

"Okay. Thanks, Mom." She pointed a finger to her cheek. He laughed and gave her a kiss, too.

~

TRAVIS LOVED the Rafter O in the winter. Although there wasn't much he could do from horseback during this time of year, he liked the clean, crisp smell in the air. He stopped on the way to the barn to take in a deep breath. There wasn't any wind, which was unusual. This felt right. Being back here and not stuck in town.

The treeless pasture stretched out to the horizon, topped with a blue sky. There wasn't a cloud in sight. No sound, except for the wind popping a loose piece of tin on the backside of the tack shed. He'd add that to his list of repairs.

His sister tapped him on the shoulder with her cap. "Quit lollygagging. Let's get to work."

"What's the forecast for this week?" They usually relied on Skip to keep them informed of any cold fronts moving in. He assumed his sister Angie would take up the helm.

"I need to check it. I don't think we're in for anything serious."

"You don't know?" He spun around and gave her a jaw-dropping look. "Aren't you in charge? What if we get caught in a norther? The cows could starve, fences are down, electricity's out. What are you gonna do then?"

She stuck out her tongue at him and pointed to the white pickup truck with the bent fender. Travis chuckled.

Angie assigned him the cookie wagon. He climbed into the feeder truck and drove to the far side of headquarters where he filled it from overhead bins with supplemental cake that they fed in the winter when the grass turned crunchy and brown. He also put several salt blocks on the back of the truck. Driving to the pasture, he admired the stark openness and even though it looked barren and dry, he knew there was a lot of wildlife during this time of year. Just to prove his point, he topped a small hill and stopped to admire a herd of antelope. They simultaneously turned their heads to look at him.

First, he had to locate the cows. Instead of spreading out like they did in the spring searching for that tender green, this time of year they stayed together in a bunch for warmth and for the cookie wagon. He spotted the first herd across a shallow ravine. He honked the horn and waited until they were close, mooing with impatience as they walked towards him. He drove a straight line and flipped a switch. The automatic feeder clinked as it dropped cow cake on the ground in neat little mounds and then he drove back by to get a count. Angie had jotted down the numbers in each pasture in a pocket notebook for him.

In a few years, Wyatt would be old enough to go with him most days. And he could hardly wait to put him in a saddle. It felt good to be back home and he looked forward to sharing all he knew with his son.

He drove from pasture to pasture, locating the cows, spreading cake, and getting a count. He didn't hate mind-numbing work. The morning passed by fast and it kept him from obsessing over his wife. Mid-afternoon his stomach growled to remind him he had skipped lunch and needed food, so he drove back to headquarters.

"There you are," Angie met him as he stepped out of the feeder truck. "This week we need to put out several big round bales for the horses, take out a grove of salt cedars in the West Pasture if you feel up to spending some time in the backhoe, unload an extra shipment of hay I lucked out in finding, sweep the barn, and maybe other stuff as I think of it." He sighed. It was going to be a long winter with his sister and her To Do lists.

"You don't have to talk to me like I'm a toddler."

"What?" She spun around, hands on hips.

"Angie, you're spouting off an endless list of work. I grew up on this ranch. I know what needs to be done. Dad may have put you in charge while he was sick and out of his head lying in a hospital bed, but you're not officially the foreman of this ranch. We work together. Deal?" He knew that he risked his relationship with Angie before he had even moved back home, but she had to stop bossing him around. She'd been doing that for as long as he could remember.

"What are you saying?"

"I'm saying that I am a married man and a father, and I don't like the way you boss me around."

First, she turned red, and then glared at him. Sudden anger lit up her eyes. And then she calmed and hung her head. In a few minutes she met his gaze.

"You're right. I have been spouting orders right and left. I'm sorry. Thanks for being here. Let's do this. Together."

He walked closer to give her a hug. "Together, we will get through this, Angie, and Dad will be okay."

She absentmindedly wiped moisture from her cheek and cleared her throat. "You missed lunch, but I think Mom saved you some leftovers. And then why don't you take off, Travis? I know you have packing to do tonight. Do you need any help?" Angie stood over him, notebook in her hand. Seemed she was always checking off lists.

"I would like to get started on it. It'll probably be a long night for me."

"Well, get going. Holler if you need anything. Tomorrow after you move your stuff in, come see me. There's always more work to do."

"Sure thing. See ya tomorrow."

Travis went to see his mother who warmed up a plate of enchiladas for him, got the flattened boxes she had, and loaded them in his truck.

Back inside he saw Kaylee playing with Wyatt.

"Come on, Wyatt. Time to go home."

"No. Kay Kay!"

"I know, buddy. You must've had fun today. Now we need to go home. Daddy's got a lot to do tonight."

Kaylee stood. "I can watch him anytime. Just let me know."

"Thanks. I appreciate that." He patted the jean pocket with his wallet. "I'll have to bring you cash tomorrow, if that's all right."

Grace picked Wyatt up. It was obvious they all were trying to avoid a meltdown.

"Let's go, little man. Meme will carry you to Dada's truck. Okay? Let's go!"

"Kay Kay!"

"Kaylee has to stay here and wash the dishes," Grace fibbed and winked at the babysitter giving her a heads up to stay inside. Out of sight, out of mind. "She'll see you tomorrow."

Travis gathered up the diaper bag and the rest of Wyatt's belongings and headed to the truck.

"Remember, any time." Kaylee smiled.

Travis made a mental note to find out what her fees were and stop by the bank. Angie was right. His priorities needed to change, and he had to face the realization that he might become a single parent.

16
TRAVIS

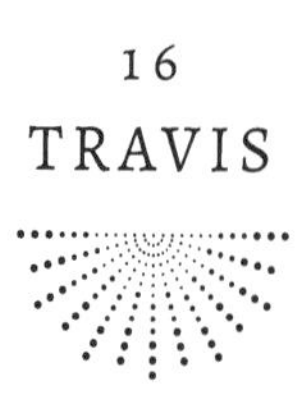

19 DAYS UNTIL CHRISTMAS

TRAVIS COULD HAVE SLEPT IN THAT MORNING, but duty called. Plus, he was more than a little afraid of facing Angie again if he was late. He had been packing his and Wyatt's stuff, and cleaning Julee Rae's house until well past midnight. The boxes were stacked neatly in the entry hall next to the front door. Probably only got a few hours of sleep. He made a fresh pot of coffee and noticed the old photo album that he had found when emptying a dresser drawer. He had tossed it on the kitchen table and then forgot to put it in a box. No one made those anymore, it was all digital nowadays. But Destynee did.

Filling a mug, he sat down and flipped through pages of memories—rodeos where Destynee was the flag bearer or singing the National Anthem in the middle of the arena. They were so young when they first got together. A few pics were of their quirky wedding in the Olsens' backyard. Was that really just a year ago?

Seemed like a lifetime. Shortly thereafter, images of their infant son howling his head off. But he was beautiful. And he was theirs. Both had contributed to his flesh and bones. Their blood ran through him. He was a gift from God.

He pushed the album away like it was poison. Travis wished he had never looked through it. Why keep tearing out his heart? He cautiously wondered if their album of life together would continue, have more pages. Wyatt in the first grade, riding a horse, playing sports, growing up, getting married. Don't even go there, man. Don't jinx everything. There was a time when he had looked into the blue eyes of his wife and seen forever. Now he wasn't so sure.

He got busy making trips outside and had packed his truck with the boxes before the sun was up. Only thing left was to wait until Wyatt woke up. He made one last sweep of the house to turn off lights, remembered to clean out the refrigerator, and took the trash bags to the curb. He made the decision to leave the crib and move Wyatt to a toddler bed his mom and dad had bought for him, so there wasn't any furniture to move. Just their clothes and toys. It truly was amazing how much stuff a baby needed.

Wyatt hollered. He scooped him up still in his pajamas, grabbed his coffee, and locked the front door after slamming it somewhat. He wanted to close this chapter of his life. He wanted to move on. Wherever that would take him.

His son was wide-eyed and curious about a truck ride so early in the morning. "Are you hungry? We'll be at Meme's in a few minutes, buddy."

Driving to the ranch he tried Destynee again. He was starting to feel as though he was just talking to himself, that no one on the other end was even hearing his messages.

"Hey. It's me. Wyatt and I are moving back to the Rafter O." He cleared his throat. He really wanted to hear her voice. "I wanted to let you know. It just makes sense. Angie needs my help, Dad is coming home from the hospital day after tomorrow. And it'll be closer for the babysitter and my mom, when she can, to take care of Wyatt while I'm working. I'm sure you're busy, but I hope you can come home soon. Wyatt misses you." He paused again. "I miss you. I love you, Destynee. Please call me back."

He set the phone down and looked out the window at the endless sky.

Wyatt was in his car seat in the back and said, "Mama?"

"Yes, Son. I was calling your Mama."

NATHAN'S TRUCK was in front of the Olsens' ranch house. Travis parked next to it and got Wyatt out of his car seat and went inside.

"Mornin'," he said, opening the door.

One after the other said, "Hey, Travis."

His mom, Nathan and wife Indya with their son Gabriel, oldest sister Janie, and babysitter Kaylee were all there.

"Wow," he said, "looks like a full house in here. What is this? An intervention or somethin'?" He put Wyatt down on the living room carpet to play with Gabe and Indya. Squeals ensued.

Grace poured coffee for those who wanted it. "No, it is not an intervention, smarty. They all wanted to help me because your dad is coming home on Thursday. Janie spent the night last night," she told Travis. "And Nathan and Indya came by this morning. Maybe Nathan can give you a hand with the boxes in your truck."

"That would be great."

"So, you're moving back in?" Nathan headed out to the truck with Travis.

"Yeah, at least for a while. Angie needs my help and it'll be easier to have Wyatt here near Mom and the babysitter."

"Any news on Destynee's return?"

Travis grunted as he hefted a box. "Uh, no, not really."

"That must be hard, man. I know you miss her."

"Yeah, well, what am I supposed to do? Gotta keep goin'. Do the right thing for Wyatt."

"Just let me know if you need anything. I mean that, Travis. Call me anytime. Don't try and do this alone."

"Thanks, bro. I appreciate it. So, what are you and Indya doin' today?"

"Well, we heard Dad is doing better and is coming home. I hope he takes it slow like the doctor said. Indya thought it would be nice to take Mom to the store. She won't have much time when Dad gets home. Kaylee can take care of the two boys. I guess you need to get to work, don't you?"

"Yeah, soon. Angie told me to get moved in and then find her for my chores list."

"You think that's going to work out? You working for Angie."

"Sure. I'm okay with it. She tells me what needs to be done and I do it. I gotta say I was exhausted yesterday. After the ranch work, last night I packed up and cleaned

Julee Rae's house. I'll probably collapse tonight after work."

"And I guess you haven't been doing 'regular' work the last few months, right?"

"You can say it, Nathan. I've been moping around. And drinking."

"All right. You said it. Do you think you're out of that funk now?"

"Well, it's only day two of work. Ask me in a month. I'm taking it one day at a time."

"Sounds like an AA slogan."

"I was probably close to going down that path, bro. I'm trying to steer clear of that stuff and get my life together."

"Like I said, I'm here for you, Travis. And I'm proud of you. You're trying to do the right thing through hard times. Indya and I will keep you and your family in our prayers."

"Thanks, Nathan. I know you and Indya pray."

"Remember, we've been through rough patches too. I think we both discovered that life is easier if we stay 'prayed up' so to speak. And if we're honest and tell each other how we're doing, what we're thinking. You know, our wants and desires. What's bothering us."

Travis grinned up at his big brother who towered over him. "You always were a sensitive guy, Nathan."

Travis laughed and jabbed him in the side. Nathan grabbed his brother in a headlock.

"Now who's sensitive, little brother? Huh? Huh?" He rubbed Travis's head hard.

Suddenly the front door opened and their mother stood with hands on her hips, but then a grin. "You two had better stop acting like you're twelve. Get those last boxes into Travis's room. Angie has already called wondering where he is."

In unison they both said, "Yes, ma'am."

After she went in, Travis chuckled and shoved his brother who cuffed his head.

They picked up the last two boxes and headed in.

"You know, Travis, you're my favorite brother."

With another shove, he answered, "I'm your only brother, jerk."

INSIDE THEY SET the last of the boxes on the floor in Travis's room.

"Hey, little brother." Janie was putting fresh sheets on his bed.

"You don't have to do that. I can make the bed later. After work."

"I have a feeling after work you're gonna just want to crash into the bed. It'll help if it's ready and waiting for you."

"Well, thanks. I appreciate it."

"No problem. I told Mom I'd help out however I can. But soon I've got to get to work. And I think you do too. Are you going to put Wyatt's crib in that corner?"

"I left his crib at Julee Rae's house. Mom and Dad got Wyatt a toddler bed. I can rearrange things later and I'll need to put the bed together."

"Travis, let me give you a tip. Don't put everything off till later. Then you just end up with a big mess, everything piled up, and you get overwhelmed. I've been there. And I'm not just talking about making your bed or setting up Wyatt's toddler bed. It holds true for relationships also. Take care of things now before they get out of control. Then it's hard to reel them back in to where they're supposed to be."

"Hmm...I guess this is big sister advice, huh?" He wasn't quite sure he wanted everyone's advice about his marriage.

"Travis, we all love you. We're just trying to help."

He threw a comforter on the bed.

"I know. And I appreciate it."

"Have you talked with Destynee? When will she be home?"

He felt himself clamming up. He couldn't keep going over this again and again. He didn't have the answers.

"I don't know, Janie. She's not returning my calls."

"Do you know her schedule? Where she's gonna be each day? What if there was an emergency with Wyatt? How would you get in touch with her?"

"I don't know, Janie." His tone was harder this time.

But she persisted. "What about social media? I'm sure her mother is promoting her...uh, uh...tour. You could find out dates and places there. Maybe show up and talk to her."

"Janie, I've got to get to work or Angie will have my hide. Thanks for your help."

He left abruptly. But took with him a seed of an idea. Maybe he would try to find out where Destynee was. After all, she was his wife. Truth was, he didn't even know if she had a website, or how Julee Rae marketed her. There had to be a social media site or contact information posted somewhere, otherwise how did they book her for a show and get people to follow her? He made a mental note to research that the first chance he got.

17
DESTYNEE

18 DAYS UNTIL CHRISTMAS

DESTYNEE STUDIED THE MENU, HER STOMACH rolling as she considered the choices: chicken, burgers, enchiladas. She had been living on power bars from her mother's snack pack for almost a month. A good meal would help her mood and motivation considerably.

The Christmas decorations had thrown her though. Moving from one show to another with a zillion costume changes in between, she hardly realized what time of year it was. This steakhouse was over the top with red and green bows, Santas and trees, and it made her sad. She should be home with her toddler son, making cookies, although she rarely spent any time in the kitchen, but that didn't mean she didn't want to. Decorating a tree. Shopping for toys. It had been a long time since she and her mother had spent Christmas at home.

"I'm having a steak," Julee Rae said. "But you'll do well to have salad so you can fit into that new dress. If you happen to increase even half a size, that wipes out over half of your performance wardrobe. Money down the drain after all the work I've put in to acquire it for you."

Annoyance washed over Destynee. She ignored her mother and stayed hidden behind the menu.

"There he is!" Julee Rae popped out of her chair and waved an arm over her head.

Destynee peeped over the menu to see a man waving back. Her annoyance expanded into a burning sensation in her gut that had nothing to do with hunger. She recognized him. "Neon Suit" had been backstage at one of her performances. Countless towns and venues ago, it seemed. She couldn't remember which. This time he wore a bright blue suit with an orange shirt and tie. His hair pulled tight against his scalp into a man bun at the back.

He sat down in the empty chair next to her.

"Ladies. So good to see you again."

"Lucius. Thank you for joining us. This is my daughter, Destynee. I don't think I've made a formal introduction."

"Your performance was extraordinary. I enjoyed it very much." He extended a hand, which Destynee shook. His hands were soft, his nails manicured, and his smile seemed genuine. Despite herself, she liked him.

She felt her cheeks warm from the compliment. "Thank you."

"I wonder if you write music too?"

"Actually, I do." She laughed. "I have songs written on napkins and—"

"He's not interested in your scribblings, Destynee. Let's order and then we can talk business."

That made Destynee perk up and wonder what this lunch was really about. Her mother was being somewhat nice. They were finally able to sit down and enjoy a good meal together for once, but she distrusted the effort. She should have known. Obviously, there was another motive. There was always another motive. It was sad that she felt that way. She had been traveling with Julee Rae for many years and knew how she manipulated everyone to do her bidding.

Destynee pretended to be indecisive about the menu, waiting until the other two had placed their orders and then she looked directly at the waitress. "I'd like a steak, please. Medium well. And a salad."

If looks could kill, but she had seen that glare on her mother's face before and she was still here on earth. Her empty stomach won over any feelings of guilt. Yes, she was acting like a spoiled child, but, at some point, her mother would have to start seeing her as a married woman with a child of her own.

"Lucius will be working with us to help your image."

"My image?" Destynee had always believed that what you see is what you get. She never put on airs or pretended to be anything other than what she was.

"Your mother thinks you might benefit from a much larger online presence. Do you have a website? Facebook page? Do you engage with any social media at all?"

"No, not really. When I'm not singing or practicing, I journal and write songs."

"Beautiful. Moody songwriter slash singer. There's a mystery about you." Lucius paused and looked into the distance over her head. "I can work with that."

"We need bigger venues and new territory. I think she's saturated the local opportunities around this state." Julee Rae cut her steak into tiny bite-sized pieces and delicately placed one in her mouth.

"Possibly. With an active social, her fans will multiply

and with that comes more. More venues. More fans." His eyes sparkled with excitement. "I see this new Destynee as an intriguing creature with an angelic voice. We want her to be a bit of a mystery."

"There's nothing that mysterious about me. I'm a new wife, I have a baby son, and I love to sing."

Destynee looked from one to the other as they talked about her as though she wasn't even there. If they asked her, which they most likely wouldn't, she was fine with traveling in the immediate area. Many of the people remembered her every year. She thought of them as family and she really enjoyed the smaller stages. She had never thought of herself singing in front of thousands of people in a stadium. That had never been a dream of hers.

"And then there's the merch."

"What?"

"Merchandise. We need to get you in the studio and cut a CD. You need a logo. We can put that on T-shirts, banners, coffee mugs." He suddenly pointed a finger inches from her face. "Do you drink coffee?"

Destynee jumped at the sudden movement. "Yes."

"Great. We might find an endorsement deal for you."

Her lunch suddenly turned bland. Her mother and Lucius kept talking and planning, pulling the strings as if she were a nameless, faceless puppet on a stage. Dread washed over her. Travis and Wyatt's faces floated in her mind and she almost burst out crying. At this rate, she may never be a part of their lives.

The meal passed with Destynee remaining silent and blocking out most of what the other two talked about. She'd find out soon enough what she had to be doing. She just wanted to get it over with so she could get home to Wyatt and Travis.

"Hand me your phone. I'll put my number in, and then you text me so I'll have your contact information."

Destynee glared at her mother who reluctantly pulled the cell phone from her own purse and handed it to Lucius. And then she took a second glance because she had never seen that purse before. Navy blue leather. Nice.

After Lucius had typed in his number, she took her phone from his hand before her mother could get it back. She texted him, and as they walked to the front of the restaurant, she checked her texts. Nothing from Travis. Her heart dropped to her knees. She couldn't believe it. No missed calls either. That explained more than she wanted to know.

Was this the beginning of the end?

18
TRAVIS

17 DAYS UNTIL CHRISTMAS

ANGIE AND GRACE LEFT FOR THE HOSPITAL TO bring Skip home, and Travis had specific instructions to rearrange the living room. If he were a betting man, he'd lay odds that his father would have him move it all back the way it is. But his mother had been hopping around like a jack rabbit, excited to have her husband back, so Travis was happy to oblige.

He moved the sofa out of the way and moved his dad's recliner in that spot, closer to his bedroom and bathroom. The side table followed, already stacked with his favorite ranching and beef trade magazines, a big lamp, and a coaster for his drink. His mother planned on cutting the caffeine for a few weeks, replaced with infused lemon water. Skip was not going to be thrilled with that news. Travis angled the television to face the chair, moved the sofa into a new spot on the opposite side of the room, and paused to admire his work.

He dropped into his father's chair and checked his

phone. Still no texts and no missed calls from his wife. He frowned, almost dialed her number but stopped. He tapped messages, typed "Call me" and then deleted it. He had left enough messages and texts over the past few days, and it irritated him to keep sending them. Obviously, she was too busy to call him back.

She could at least give him an idea of where she was. He thought about calling his mother-in-law, but she never answered her phone either. He still hadn't done a search online yet. Maybe one evening he might remember, but Wyatt demanded a lot of attention from his father. Travis wondered if it was because his mother wasn't here.

The boy still muttered "Mama, sing" on occasion, usually around bedtime, and it tore at Travis's heart every time. Destynee used to sing to her baby and it was the most wonderful sound in the world. That's why Travis knew it was the right thing to do when he told her to hit the road this fall and sing. She was too talented to stay in Dixon for the rest of her life. She should share her gift with other families.

Going outside he stacked enough logs on one arm to fill the fireplace, but before he could get the fire started, he heard Wyatt.

"Did you have a good nap?" As Travis was about to lift him out of the playpen, Wyatt heaved himself up and over. "How did you learn how to do that?"

Another milestone Destynee was missing.

Wyatt walked into the living room and proceeded to pull out every toy in the basket, with Travis following along behind picking them up. He was amazed to think that it wasn't too long ago that Wyatt had taken his first steps.

"We're home," Grace called out.

Skip stopped at the threshold. "What happened in here?"

"We thought you might need to be closer to the bathroom, so I had Travis rearrange the room for you."

Skip frowned but eased into his recliner.

Grace appeared from the kitchen with a tall covered glass of ice water, straw included.

"Where's my coffee?"

Travis couldn't hide his grin when Angie walked up beside him.

"How many days before I have to move it all back?" he asked in a low voice.

"I give it two weeks," she said.

"Bet me. I'm giving it two days."

"You're on. Cash?" She raised an eyebrow.

"Nope. Loser has to help Mom in the kitchen with the dishes."

"I don't even live here."

"But you're over here all the time, and you eat most every meal here."

"I didn't want them to eat alone, since all the kids flew the coop."

"Maybe they wanted to eat alone." Travis held out his hand. "Deal?"

"Okay, fine." She shook. "You're on."

"What are you two mumbling about?" Grace faced them both, with hands on hips.

"Nothing. Is everything arranged to suit you?" Travis asked.

"It doesn't suit *me*. Not one bit." Skip raised his voice which made Wyatt look up from his toy pile.

Travis and Angie exchanged a grin.

"Mom. Wyatt can climb out of his playpen now."

"I'm not surprised. That's why I bought the toddler

bed. He is turning into a busy, busy boy." She leaned over Skip. "Do you need anything, dear? Supper will be ready in a few minutes."

"I'd take a cup of coffee."

Grace ignored his request which made Travis chuckle. His mother turned her gaze upon him. "Now that your father is home and since Wyatt can crawl out of his playpen and seems to be walking around more, you and I have a new project."

"Oh, yeah?" Travis smiled because at least he'd have something else to keep him busy and maybe he could avoid some of his sister's bossy attitude. Angie was turning into a micro-manager and he was becoming more and more annoyed with her. "Whatever you need me to do, Mom. That's one of the reasons I moved back home, to help y'all. What are we doing?"

"Potty training."

19
TRAVIS

16 DAYS UNTIL CHRISTMAS

WEATHER IN TEXAS HAS A MIND OF ITS OWN. Yesterday—hot as Hades when he moved all those boxes to the Rafter O. And today an overcast sky with wind straight from the north, a reminder that it was still mid-December. He had lived here his whole life and he never tired of experiencing the four seasons. Each unique and distinct, with a new set of challenges.

Whatever the forecast, he could still exercise a couple of horses for Angie in the enclosed arena. Keep them conditioned, she had said. There was one that had been giving him a little trouble. Liked bucking. That wasn't a good thing for ranch work. But Travis knew how to cure him of it.

The horse was fine being saddled so Travis got him ready and headed into a round pen. He shortened the inside rein and secured it to the saddlehorn and let the horse go, its body curved to the left. Travis encouraged him to run. The horse soon found out he couldn't buck so easily with his torso bent and his head facing to the left.

"Better to get the kinks out before you get on him." A familiar voice sounded and Travis looked in that direction.

"Buck Wallace. How are you?"

"Doin' well. How ya been, Travis?"

"Oh, pretty good. Just doin' what I'm told."

"That's all ya can do. Keeps you outta trouble."

Both men laughed. Travis came over to shake the older man's weathered hand. Buck was foreman of the neighboring Wild Cow Ranch and had been a family friend of the Olsens since before Travis was born.

"How's your dad doin'? I hear he's out of the hospital."

"Yes, he got home yesterday. He's doing a lot better. You should go inside and see him."

"I hate to bother him since he just got home. I'll be back." Buck leaned one arm across the top railing. "That was some wreck, I hear."

"It happened so fast, he's lucky to be alive. Wish I had done more."

"Travis, I'm sure you did all that you could under the circumstances. It was an accident."

As they leaned on the fence and watched the horse go round and round, Travis tried to put into words what had happened. It still haunted him and he always choked up when he tried to tell it. When the horse slowed down, Travis egged him on some more. Keep 'em moving, his dad had always told him. If he's going forward, he can't be bucking.

"It's just that I felt like I froze. Nathan was the one who stayed calm and gave us all instructions. Dad was out cold."

"I'm sure what was probably a nanosecond of shock felt like an hour to you. They say things slow down in times of crisis. It's hard to see one of our loved ones hurt. I think God slows down our mind to protect us."

"I don't know about that. I just hate letting my dad down."

"I'm sure you didn't. Sounds like everyone jumped in to call the paramedics and rush him to the hospital. Don't be so hard on yourself, man. You did the right thing. Let's just be glad God spared his life."

"You're right, Buck. I sure am glad of that."

"I saw that little feller of yours out front with the babysitter gettin' something out of her car. He sure is growing like a weed. You know, we're going to have a Live Nativity again this year at the Wild Cow. The little kids will be able to ride the donkey. He's gentle enough. Ya oughta bring Wyatt by."

"When is it?"

Buck sheepishly said, "Tomorrow. Years ago it was always the first Saturday in December. After Carli inherited the Wild Cow from her grandfather and became the new owner, we have it mid-December. I'm here to ask a few neighbors for a little help. I spoke to Angie on the phone earlier. We still have a lot to do to be ready for the whole community to come out and visit."

"Sure. What can I help you with?"

"I wonder if I can borrow you and your trailer. I need a load of sheep picked up for the manger area. The boss lady wants to have a petting zoo of some sort."

"Sure. I can do that."

"You know Shannon out on County Road D? It's his sheep, and then he'll be there tomorrow night with his sheep dogs. He just needs transport for the flock tomorrow morning."

"Sure, I can help with the sheep. And I'll try to bring Wyatt to the Open House. He loves animals. And if Dad's feeling up to it, maybe he can come too. I don't think he and mother ever missed an Open House at the Wild Cow in the olden days. I remember them talking about it."

"How about Destynee? Will she be home from the road?"

Travis's pursed mouth scrunched to the side and he shook his head. "Buck, I'm not sure. I've been trying to get a hold of her but haven't had much luck."

Buck hesitated, then said, "She must be real busy. Don't worry, Travis. I'm sure she'll make it home in time for Christmas. And probably with a carload of presents for her little boy." With a wink and a big laugh, he added, "And maybe one for you, *IF* you've been a good boy."

"I hope she makes it home, Buck. I sure hope so."

Travis walked to the middle of the pen. "I think it's time this fella went the other way." He loosened the reins, shortened the right one so that the head was nearly turned around to the horse's side. It didn't hurt him. Only made him think. One day he would come to the realization that Travis was his leader and, most importantly, that bucking was a very bad idea. Travis clicked his tongue and slapped his thigh to encourage the horse to move.

Angie appeared and walked up next to their neighbor. "Hey, Buck, good to see you. Are you telling Travis what kind of help you need for your Christmas social tomorrow?" They shared a laugh and Buck put an arm around her shoulder for a hug hello. She looked at Travis. "I volunteered you. Did he tell you?"

"That's what I hear. Mostly we've been chewing the fat and watching this horse go 'round." He grinned.

"Hmmm." She gave him a playful stern face, then changed it to a smile and shake of her head. "How much longer with this horse, Travis? I've got some other things that need to be done before your day is done."

"Maybe thirty more minutes. I'd like to get on him for at least a few minutes before I put him up. See if the attitude adjustment worked."

"All right. Do what you need to do. Find out what Buck needs for their event. Then come see me."

Angie walked away and the two men got back to watching the horse. Every so often Travis made smooching sounds to get the horse moving again when it dawdled.

"So, what else can I help you with, Buck?"

"Well, as you know, the Wild Cow Christmas Open House is for the whole community. All the ladies make a ton of cookies to be passed out. And the lights. Wow. Lights on every building of the ranch. On the fences. Everywhere. Last year the power went out due to an ice storm. So, we always have to think of a backup plan just in case. Usually, people come out no matter what the weather."

"Oh, right. I remember the lanterns."

"Carli found those in the basement. They were antiques from her grandfolks. We attached those darn things to every fence post or set them on the ground. It was a lot of work but it sure did look pretty when we got done."

"Hopefully, this year you won't lose power."

"Yeah, hope not. It's such a fun event and the townsfolk love coming out. We went a lot of years without having the Open House. Then Carli brought it back even bigger and better."

"Cool. So, what do you need from me?"

"Lucky for you, we already put the lights up last month. That was a huge job. I need some help on the Nativity shed, if you have time after you deliver the sheep. I have some of it left over from last year but it was dismantled for storing so now it needs a little carpentry work to put it back together. It's like a little house with a pen around it for the animals."

"When do you want me to come by?"

"Early, if you have time. After you run by Shannon's place."

"Sure. I've got nothing else going on."

"Bring Wyatt with you, too."

"Oh, I don't know. If I'm gonna be working…"

"Nonsense. I know Lola would love to get her hands on that little guy. I'll ask her to make sure, if that'll make you feel better. I'll text you. How's that?"

"You know how to text?"

Buck grabbed Travis's shoulders. "Watch it, you rascal. I'm not as old as I look."

Travis chuckled. "That must be why you ended up with Lola for your wife. She wouldn't be with some old geezer."

"Probably some truth in that, smart aleck." Buck let out a hearty laugh.

Travis walked over to the horse and untied the reins. He checked the cinch.

"Good thing you're here in case he decides to dump me." He grinned at Buck. "But I think he's worn out."

Putting one boot in the stirrup he carefully swung his other leg over the saddle and sat still. The horse was quiet and Travis nudged him to trot. No problem. He reined him back the other way. Still relaxed. After riding ten or more minutes, he decided that was enough for one day.

"I think we'll end on a good note." Travis halted the horse and dismounted. Loosened the saddle and led him towards the barn.

"You've got a calm way around horses," Buck said.

"It's the only way to be. My dad taught me."

"I think he taught all of his kids a lot of good things. Love, patience, respect. The same traits that can be used with people. Another one is honesty. Tell the horse what you want. Tell people what you want."

Travis looked into Buck's eyes. He knew Buck was giving him a message, a life lesson. He remembered receiving them as a kid. And most times, Buck was right.

20
TRAVIS

"Mom, I have a few things to finish up here because I need to get over to the Wild Cow early tomorrow and help Buck and Lank. Can we shop another day?" Travis was about to dive into a bowl of stew. The smell made his stomach rumble.

"Whatever it is can wait. You need to do a little Christmas shopping for Wyatt. This is going to be an exciting Christmas for him. And have you shopped for your siblings?"

Travis shrugged. "I'll give them money." He looked to his dad who sat next to him at the kitchen bar, but Skip focused on putting butter on a square of cornbread.

"You can't give Wyatt money!"

"Why don't you pick him out a nice toy and I'll pay you?"

She stared daggers at him.

"You have got to be kidding me, Travis Ethan Olsen. You're his father. You pick the toy. Wyatt was only a couple of months old for his first Christmas so he wouldn't remember that. But this is the first Christmas he *will* remember."

A gust of cold air followed Angie in through the back door as she walked over to the stove and filled a bowl for herself. She didn't interrupt her mother's rant. Instead, she gave Travis a big wide grin from behind her mother's back.

Help me, he mouthed when Grace turned to face the sink.

Angie shook her head and mouthed, *No Way.*

All of the Olsen siblings had mixed emotions about going shopping with Grace. The chaos, the traffic, and each one of them had gotten lost at one time or another. She wanted them all to experience the joys of the season. His sister Libbie was the shopper in the family and she was spending Christmas with one of her Baylor roommates.

Grace continued. "We've been talking to him about Santa and Jesus and about giving gifts to one another. So, we are going shopping. I've already told Angie that you're going with me. Kaylee will come by to watch Wyatt."

She glanced at her husband. Skip cleared his throat. "I better stay here and rest."

"I'll keep an eye on Dad. Make sure he has everything he needs," Angie offered.

"And I think Wyatt and I will do just fine on our own," Skip said. "You can call Kaylee and tell her not to come. That'll save him a few bucks."

Travis started to open his mouth when one look from his mother cut him short. "Not one word," she said.

"Fine."

While they ate lunch, Angie brought her father up to speed on everything she and Travis had been doing that morning. Travis could tell that his father was going stir crazy. The frustration was evident in his eyes. He really wanted to be back outside but if he stepped one foot onto a horse, Grace would have his hide. And if Skip Olsen went outside, he'd find some reason or another to be on a horse.

"Have fun little brother," Angie said on her way out the door. She didn't stifle the giggle that followed.

THEY DROVE in relative silence to Amarillo, Travis's jaw clenched in frustration. An hour to the city, shopping for who knows how long, and the drive back. That's an afternoon he won't be on the payroll so it didn't make sense for him to be spending money he didn't have.

As they approached the city Grace's excitement was almost palpable. "I know you must be missing Destynee, but maybe shopping for your son will pick up your spirits." She looked over to Travis as he drove. "The lights, the decorations, and the spirit of the season. Really gets you in the mood, doesn't it?"

"Mmm huh," was all he came up with. His mother had a way of cutting right to the quick. Missing his wife had nothing to do with buying toys. And besides, Wyatt's mother should be at his side shopping for toys instead of his grandmother. His mood grew darker. He had given up on leaving voicemails and texts for his wife. Destynee had not replied even once. He couldn't help but wonder if everything was all right. On top of his frustration of unanswered calls, he now added worry for her safety.

"Oh, Travis, you're acting like a real Scrooge. I hope

you get out of this dark mood soon so you don't ruin Wyatt's Christmas."

He just rolled his eyes and waited patiently in the traffic. They had sat through this same light three times. He watched happy shoppers. Christmas used to be his favorite holiday. Would he ever be happy again?

"Where to?" He wanted to park and get this over with as soon as possible.

"Let's go to the farm and ranch store first. They have some tractors for toddlers that I want to look at. Wyatt needs jeans and western shirts, if I can find his size. Wonder if they have chaps? What do you have in mind?"

"I dunno, Mom."

"Well, you'll find something he will like."

Inside the store things were bustling with more happy families, some with two parents, some single mothers or fathers. Travis stopped to admire a giant Christmas tree decorated with duck calls, truck ornaments, and tons of tractor ornaments. Santas on tractors, snowmen riding tractors, and some were printed with kids' names.

Grace led the way through the lawn and garden, bird seed, and equine sections to the toys. Travis tried to avoid eye contact as best he could, as some people said "Hello" and "Merry Christmas." Typical Texas Panhandle. It almost made him sick. They must be faking it. No one could be that happy.

"Travis! Over here. Wyatt would love this." It was hard for his mother to contain her enthusiasm.

As he made his way to the aisle where Grace had stopped, he stared at a giant stuffed horse with brown and white patches, a little fake leather saddle, fake leather reins, and silver plastic stirrups. It was about three times the size of Wyatt.

"That's not a tractor," he said.

"I love this!" His mother was nearly beside herself. "Don't you just love it? You could get him this."

"How would we get it in the truck? How would we wrap it? It's too big."

"It will fit in the back of the cab just fine, or maybe you can tie it down in the back."

"Mom, settle down." He looked at other shoppers around them.

"Okay, I'm sorry, Travis. But you've got to pull yourself out of this slump and think about your son."

"Fine," he grumbled. "Get the horse."

"And this." She stood in front of a green John Deere tractor that was Wyatt's size, which Travis had to admit, was perfect. Grace literally did a little hop and quietly clapped her hands in front of her face.

"Oh, good. You'll be glad when you see Wyatt's face as he unwraps this on Christmas morning. Which one do you want to buy? I'll buy the other one."

"Whatever you say."

She looked around for a salesclerk. "I'll find someone to help us with the horse and tractor, but I need to get some other things. Some building blocks. A little piano. Maybe an action figure. I hear they're bringing that one back with the stretchy arms. Oh, and while we're here, I should pick up some toys for Gabriel. I've been shopping for months, but you can never have enough when it comes to Christmas for kids."

Travis watched his mother. She was the epitome of the phrase, "kid in a candy store" and there was no slowing her down. As much of a Jesus follower as she was, Grace also loved the commercial side of Christmas.

"And the bookstore. I want to buy the boys some Bible storybooks. And Travis, you better buy extra rope so that you can tie down this stuff in the back of the pickup truck. I'm sure they sell rope here."

As he made his way towards the front of the store, he stopped at the tree. Just maybe. And there it was. A tractor ornament with *Wyatt* printed across it. He snapped a picture of it. And there was one with *Gabriel.* The luck of finding both.

He texted the picture to Destynee.

We miss you.

He hesitated, not knowing what to say next. Instead of writing anything else, he hit Send. As a store clerk pushed a cart up the narrow aisle carrying two tractors and a horse towards the front, Travis couldn't help thinking about Wyatt sitting on that tractor. He'd put the horse in front of the fireplace in the family room where they all stayed every evening.

Grace followed behind the cart. "I have two grandsons, so I had to get two tractors of course. I'll buy those and you pay for the horse. Stay there by our stuff, while I run over here to look for jeans for the boys. I'll be right back."

"Fine," he grumbled. But he didn't let his mother see the smile on his face.

21
TRAVIS

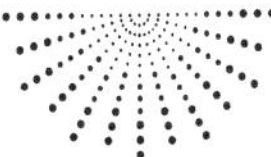

15 DAYS UNTIL CHRISTMAS

TRAVIS HAD THE TRAILER HITCHED AND everything almost ready to pull out of the Rafter O headquarters, when a text pinged on his phone.

Lola says bring Wyatt today. She'll watch him. Lank's nephew's here, too.

Skip had followed his son outside to help before Grace knew that he had slipped out. The air was crisp and of course Skip didn't have a coat on. Usually, Travis wouldn't even notice a thing like that. Now he debated whether to say anything to his father. Skip Olsen was one stubborn man. Travis decided to give his dad a break.

"Wyatt and I shouldn't be too long. And then if you feel up to it, we can go back to the Open House tonight."

"Are you sure you won't need the thirty-two-foot?" Skip asked.

"I think the twenty-four-foot will be fine. I just have to load a few sheep. Plus, Shannon has his dogs. It should go easy with their help."

"Humm. Was that Buck here yesterday?" His dad kicked the block from under the jack stand and leaned against the bed of the pickup truck.

"Yes, sir." Travis locked the clasp around the trailer ball and connected the tail light wiring. "He's enlisted several of the neighbors to help this year. I'm glad they're working together to bring this event back."

"Well, you tell Buck something for me."

Travis turned to listen to his father's harsh voice.

"You tell him I'm offended. He didn't even knock on the door to say hello to me."

"Yes, sir. I'll do that." Travis laughed. "Hop in and let's go get Wyatt."

BACK IN THE kitchen his mother giggled when he told her about the message. "He's kidding, Travis."

Regardless, Travis felt he owed more explanation. "We were busy with that horse, Dad. And then Buck had to leave."

"Angie said you guys were just blabbing."

"You know that sometimes half the work with horses is pondering and giving them time to figure things out. You taught me that."

Grace looked at her husband. "I guess he's got you there, hon."

His father cracked a smile and they all laughed. "Well, let me hold that grandson of mine for a while before you go. Come here, Wyatt. Pappy has some hugs for you."

Grace lifted the boy from his highchair and placed him in Skip's arms.

"Travis, maybe I should go with you. Wyatt hasn't seen Lola and Buck in a while. Besides, I have some cookies to drop off for their Open House tonight. Wyatt and I won't stay long. That way you can work. Maybe Angie can come get me."

His mother knew a lot about kids. He was certainly thankful to have her support and help with Wyatt. If Destynee were here, she probably would know too about the toddler going to the neighbor's. A mother's sixth sense.

"Who's gonna watch Dad while you're gone?" Travis called out to her as she disappeared into her room.

"I don't need any watching. For gosh sakes." Skip said it more under his breath to no one in particular, a pinched expression on his face.

"I'm sure Kaylee could come over for a little while. She's just down the road." Grace called out from the other room.

"I do *not* need a babysitter," his father grumbled and then he tickled Wyatt who giggled.

Travis listened to his parents with amusement. If he were a betting man, he'd guess that Skip was going to win this round. He had gotten bolder the longer he stayed inside to "rest up", as his mother called it, because she was not going to any funeral before Christmas.

"Skip, she'll just give you some lunch. She needs the money and I'll be back before you know it." Grace appeared back in the living room wearing a coat.

"What about Angie? Why can't she give me lunch?"

"I didn't want to bother her. But I guess I could ask her. Maybe she could do some of her paperwork here in the office."

"Yeah," his father said. "That'd be better than hiring a *babysitter*." He made a sour face and emphasized the word "baby" as if it was a spoiled piece of food in his mouth.

"Mom, I think Wyatt will be fine with Lola. No need to make a big fuss."

"It's no big deal. Let me just give Angie a call."

She found her cell phone and walked towards the kitchen.

Travis looked at his dad who was shaking his head back and forth to Wyatt's delight. "She just fusses too much, don't you think, Wyatt? Meme is a fusser." Then he stuck out his tongue and made a raspberry sound. Wyatt giggled and stuck out his miniature tongue.

"Oh, great, Skip. Is that something new you're teaching Wyatt?" Grace came back with a half-serious look. "Angie said she'll be over in a few minutes. She'll make calls and do her paperwork here. And get your lunch."

Skip whispered in Wyatt's little ear. "Meme is a fusser." The boy laughed and wiggled when his grandpa tickled his tummy.

"Skip Olsen, if he ever repeats that when he starts talking, you will be grounded. Mark my words."

He smothered the boy with hugs and smooches. "We're just playing, Meme. Aren't we, Wyatt?"

Wyatt laid back in Skip's arms and giggled like he'd never end. Soon his face was red and he started coughing.

"Sit him up straight and pat his back," Grace said.

Travis got closer to his son's face and stroked his arm. "You're okay, buddy. Take a breath."

Skip held the boy up straight. "He's fine. We just got excited."

After a few more coughs, Wyatt looked at Travis, confused. A half smile, but then a look of fear crossed his little face. "I think he got scared. You're okay, buddy. Want Daddy to hold you?"

Wyatt held his arms out and tears came. Travis took him from Skip.

"There ya go. You're fine, buddy. Let's load up. We're gonna go see a donkey. Won't that be fun? What sound does he make? Eeyore, Eeyore!"

Wyatt gave a genuine smile then. He knew all the animals from his storybooks.

"We should keep an eye on him today," Grace said. "Hope he's not coming down with anything."

"He's fine, Grace." Skip shook his head.

The door opened and Angie called out. "I'm here. Where's my patient?"

"He's an ornery patient today. You might have your hands full." Grace crinkled her nose at her husband.

Travis liked seeing them going back and forth at each other. It made him wonder what he and Destynee would be like at that age, but at this point it was difficult to predict how their life together would turn out. Would they even be together?

WITH WYATT LOADED in his car seat and his mother buckled in the passenger side, they took a short drive to Shannon's place, about fifteen miles to the south of the Rafter O. A drive that was anything but peaceful. His mother had bombarded him with a zillion questions the entire way about everything under the sun. He let her ramble on without answering, and finally they had arrived.

He drove down a tree-lined drive, around a rock house, and spotted sheep crowded into a pen. Two beautiful black and white sheep dogs watched with wagging tails as he backed the trailer up. But it wasn't just a few sheep, he noticed as he walked around to the back of the trailer.

"Morning!" A man with his hands stuck into blue denim overalls made his way through the flock and walked up to Travis.

Travis returned the greeting and shook the outstretched hand that reached through the fence.

"This is more than a few."

"They're all gentle and the kids will have fun petting them. If you swing those doors open, I'll get the dogs to load them for you."

The dogs did their job, guided by a few whistles and hand gestures. They were amazing to watch. Shannon walked around the passenger side of the truck to say hello to Grace, and then they were on their way again. They should arrive at the Wild Cow Ranch in another thirty minutes.

"Everyone all set?" Travis asked. "We're ready to go."

"Yes, we're good," Grace said.

"How about you, Wyatt? Are you good?" Travis turned to look at his son in the back. Wide-eyed and taking every sight and sound in, he grinned at his father.

"Sheep, bye-bye," he said and waved his hand.

Grace laughed. "We've been practicing."

22
TRAVIS

TRAVIS PULLED INTO THE WILD COW RANCH headquarters and parked near the corral. He could see fences set up on the grass, but wasn't sure where the sheep would go.

They all piled out of the pickup truck and entered the two-story cookhouse.

Lola met them at the door. "Come in!"

The dining hall ceiling reached the full two-story with a commercial kitchen tucked in one corner, under the second floor which served as apartments for Buck and Lola. Instead of feeding a room full of cowboys, this morning the dining room had been turned into a cookie bakeshop. Platters of cookies covered every table. Smells of cinnamon and butter greeted them as they walked into the room.

"Grace! So nice to see you. It's been a little while. Come on in." Lola was all smiles. "And get that little guy inside. It's starting to get pretty chilly out there. And who is this little fellow?" Lola knelt down on her knees and smiled at Wyatt. "You are growing big like your daddy."

The ranch owner Carli stuck her head out from the kitchen. "Y'all come on in. I've got cookies coming out of the oven, but make yourselves at home." She disappeared.

"I thought I'd come over and say hello." Grace held out a platter wrapped in foil. "And here's my contribution for your event. But I've got to get back to Skip before too long. Angie's with him now. She can pick me up. I can't stay."

"Thank you, we appreciate that. As you can see, we've been busy."

"I hear you had record turnout last year," Travis said.

"Yes, the community really enjoys it." Lola placed a hand on Grace's shoulder. "We were so sorry to hear about Skip's accident. I hope he's recovering."

"He's doing a lot better, thanks." Then turning to Buck, she teased. "He's a little mad at you."

"Me? What for?" Buck shrugged his shoulders.

"You didn't come in to see him when you were watching me work that horse yesterday," Travis piped up.

Buck laughed. "Well, then, I sure had better stop in and see the old geezer next time I'm out your way. Tell him I said to get well and to stop being so sensitive."

Grace smiled. "I know Skip would like that. You are both welcome anytime."

Just then two boys ran into the room. "Remember Matt Junior and Zane? They're Lank's nephews." Lola was all smiles.

"You boys are a lot taller from the last time I saw you," Grace said. "It's nice to see you."

The older one stood straight and tall. "Thank you. It's nice to see you, too."

"Very polite. I like that." Grace smiled, then led Wyatt to stand in front of her. "This is Wyatt. He's eighteen months now, going on two."

"Zane and Junior, in a few minutes we're going to take Wyatt out to see the donkey. Will you help us with that?"

"Yes, ma'am," they answered Lola.

"We're going to work on the native house." Seven-year-old Zane spoke up.

His older brother by a couple of years, Matt Junior, corrected him. "It's called a manger, and a Nativity when you put baby Jesus in there."

Wyatt hid partially behind Grace's legs. She kept her hand on his shoulder.

"Where do you want those sheep unloaded? Looks like we have a good crew of helpers." Travis said to Buck.

"Come on outside and I'll show you. I think we'll set up the petting zoo in the corral." Buck led the way towards the door.

"After you get that done, I'll bring Wyatt out," Grace said.

THE TRADITION of the Wild Cow Ranch holiday Open House went back several generations and the small town looked forward to it every year until both owners passed. Carli inherited the ranch and was trying to revive some of the community events that her great-grandparents and grandparents had hosted through the years. Tradition was vitally important to a community. Sometimes it was the glue that held it together.

Travis noticed that the arrangement was a little different than it had been in years past. There seemed to be way more lights, large ornaments hung from the trees, and Carli had added a living Nativity. What was to be the manger, Travis assumed, now lay in a heap of wood within a fenced area. It was a cool idea. Travis wondered at how many helpers it would take to keep the animals in line.

He climbed into his truck and backed the trailer up to the pipe rail fence, as close as he could. One nephew held the gate to the pens open. The other opened the trailer gate and held it back. Buck and Lank supervised.

The sheep were scared and hesitated, so Travis stepped up into the trailer to encourage them out. They exploded into the pen in one wooly mass, nearly running Lank over.

Travis laughed.

"Dang. They sure are excited," Lank said. "And that's way more than I expected."

"This is what his dogs ran into the trailer. There must be at least a dozen. I hope they settle down and kids can get close enough to pet them." Travis shut the trailer gates.

Lank shut the pen gate and then turned to look at the flock which huddled in one corner.

"Is that a llama you've got?" Travis just noticed the creature standing in the opposite corner from the sheep. Solid white, it studied them with a calm, curious demeanor.

Before Lank could answer, the hee-haws of a donkey broke the silent morning.

"There's the donkey Buck mentioned." Travis decided against disturbing the llama and walked towards the donkey instead.

"That's Eeyore. And the llama is named Mayola."

"What else are you expecting?"

"Some goats, a few miniature horses, and an English sheepdog. We'll get geared up right after lunch and people will start arriving soon after. Are y'all coming back tonight?"

"We plan on it. I hope Dad can come, too."

"How's he doing?"

"Better than expected."

Lank cleared his throat. "Can he walk okay? Good memory?"

"Yeah. I know what you're asking. I was worried about that, too. He has a little shuffle to his walk. He doesn't remember the accident. The last thing he remembers is throwing the loop."

"He was out cold. I'd never imagine anyone could have walked away from a wreck like that."

Travis swallowed the lump in his throat. "My dad is one lucky cowboy. God was watching out for him for sure."

"Maybe I should have cut the line sooner." Lank shook his head. "If I had been a split second faster."

"We were all taken by surprise. I've run it over and over in my mind, too. I think we handled it."

"I heard Destynee came by the hospital."

"Yeah. She did." Travis didn't add anything more.

"Carli and I may try to go to one of her performances, if there are any tickets left. We hear she's having sellout crowds." Lank unlatched the gate so they could pass back through.

"Yeah," was the only thing Travis could answer because he didn't want to admit that he didn't even know where his wife was singing. And tickets? He'd have to buy a ticket to see his own wife perform?

"What can I help y'all with next?" Travis asked in an effort to change the subject.

"I think the Nativity will need a lot of work."

"That pile of lumber I saw in the yard? Let's get to it then."

Travis and the nephews followed Lank to the front yard, and Buck was already there sorting through the boards. They made quick work of it. Before long a shed was finished, open on one side complete with hay bales. Ready for the animals. As much as he had been fighting it, Travis was beginning to get more and more in the Christmas spirit.

"I'm going to check on our petting zoo. I hope everyone gets along," said Lank.

"Let's go inside and sample some of those cookies." Buck grinned, and Travis and the nephews followed him back inside.

23
TRAVIS

WYATT'S LITTLE FINGERS STARTED UNZIPPING and pulling at his jacket front.

"No, no, Wyatt. Leave it on. We're going outside to see Eeyore." Grace hurriedly covered his hands and rezipped the jacket.

He coughed and fussed a little, grunting. "Uh, uh, no, Meme."

"Are you hot, baby?" She touched his forehead.

"He's fine, Mom." Travis came in and picked his son up. "Come on, everyone go outside."

"All right, all right. But let's keep an eye on him."

Lola came next to Grace and touched her elbow. "Don't worry. I'll watch him and let you know if he's not feeling well. Maybe he just got warm in the house or excited to see the animals."

"He had a coughing fit earlier when Skip was tickling him."

The two ladies followed Travis, Buck, and the nephews out to the corral.

Zane raced ahead of the others. “We want to show Wyatt the donkey.”

“Slow down, partner. I haven’t even said hello to our visitors.” Lank nodded and smiled towards Grace. “Kids, right? Full of energy.”

Grace hugged Lank. “Haven’t seen you in a while. How are you? I saw your wife inside, surrounded by cookies.”

“We’re doing fine. Yeah, she’s making more cookies, like we really need any more, and probably rummaging in the basement for more decorations. You know she likes to make Christmas a big deal now. Making up for the past, I guess.”

“It was wonderful last year,” Grace said.

“We’d like to show Wyatt the donkey.” Lola said.

“Is that a llama?” Grace stopped in her tracks, mouth wide open.

Everyone shared a laugh at the shocked look on her face.

They walked around to the pen towards the donkey.

“Is he yours?” Travis asked.

Lank grabbed a halter. “He’s kind of on loan for Christmas from Miss Vera down the road. He’s pretty docile which makes it great when a lot of kids want to pet or ride on him.”

“Look, Wyatt. It’s Eeyore. Want to pet him?” Grace was in full on grandma mode.

Wide-eyed and enthralled with the animals, Wyatt was shy at first and held back. “Dada.” He reached for Travis and pointed to the llama, his head swiveling from one to the other.

“Come on, buddy. Eeyore is nice. You’re a cowboy, aren’t ya?”

Zane came forward and petted the donkey's neck and stroked his long ears. "Look, Wyatt, he's friendly. We'll stand right next to you."

Lank smiled and waited with the halter. "Good boy, Zane. Help him out."

Travis held his son and lowered him to reach through the fence to pet the animal with his tiny fingers. Soon Wyatt was giggling and appeared more comfortable. "Eeyore."

Lola asked, "Do you think he'd like to sit on the donkey? I could take some pictures with my phone."

"Let's try it." Grace nodded. "Take a picture, Travis."

Lank opened the gate and led the donkey out by its halter. "Zane, do you want to just sit on him to show Wyatt he doesn't need to be scared?"

"Sure, Unc."

They lined up the donkey next to the fence and Zane crawled up the boards to get on top of him.

"You're getting big so just sit for a minute. You can't ride him."

When Wyatt saw the boy atop the donkey he broke out in a big smile. "Me, me! Eeyore!"

"All right, buddy. Hold on. Wait your turn." After Zane slid off, Travis raised Wyatt over the donkey and placed him on its back, holding onto him the whole time.

Wyatt giggled and started to kick his legs.

"Ride 'em, cowboy," Lank said. "Let's go out into the pen for a while. Travis, get on the other side and hold onto him as I lead Eeyore."

"Smile, Wyatt!" Lola took pics with her phone.

"What a big boy!" Grace beamed.

As Wyatt got more and more comfortable, he petted the donkey's neck and gave the two ladies his biggest smile. Soon he kicked his little legs which didn't bother the donkey at all. Travis snapped a few pictures.

"Yeehaw! You're a natural, Wyatt!" Lank grinned at Travis. "You've got a little bronc rider on your hands!"

24
DESTYNEE

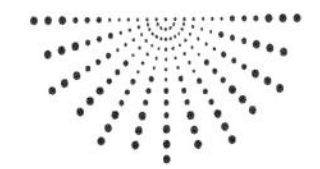

15 DAYS UNTIL CHRISTMAS

THEY HAD WORKED THEIR WAY BACK ACROSS the middle of Texas, farther away from her husband and son, and they were now parked in downtown Dallas in the warehouse district.

"Are you sure this is the right address?" Destynee was driving while her mother studied the map on her phone.

"Go that way and let's look for other vehicles." She pointed. "There, there. That must be them."

"How many people are supposed to be here?"

"I don't know Destynee. Lucius has his team that he works with and it's going to take a team of people to turn you into a star. It's all an illusion, ya know. He says to bring your guitar."

Great. So now she was supposed to be play-acting as being some big star. She didn't want to be an illusion, she just wanted to sing her songs.

She parked next to the other cars and they walked through the only metal door located on that side of the massive brick building. Inside, she gasped. Light poured in from one wall of windows, illuminating curved, cement steps with a broken iron railing. Dirt coated everything. The walls, the floors, the windowsills. More light from a giant hole in the roof cast a shimmer on a puddle of water.

Ragged, rusted tiles hung from the ceiling above, and the entire space was dotted with giant cement pillars. The faint odor of dust mixed with mold and stagnant water did not make for a pleasant atmosphere. How was she supposed to pose for photos in this rundown dump?

"Ladies! Come in!" Lucius spread his arms wide. "Don't you love it?"

"It's fabulous, darling," said Julee Rae. "I just love it to pieces."

Destynee had to turn her head to look at her mother. Since when had she lost her Texas accent? She sounded like she was from the California coast.

"You can get dressed behind that screen in the far corner. We have everything laid out. Put on all the pieces in each group."

Next to him stood a woman with a camera, a teenaged girl dressed all in black, and a young man holding a reflector. Destynee walked across the cement floor, her shoes echoing in the empty space.

Behind the screen she discovered three piles of clothes along with shoes. She chose a leather skirt, pink frilly shirt, and tall brown boots. But when she pulled the boots on, they came just above her knee and the skirt was way shorter.

"Bring your guitar," Lucius called out.

Destynee stepped out from behind the screen. "This skirt doesn't fit."

"Yes, it looks perfect."

"My behind is barely covered."

"No worries. We're not photographing your backside. Step here next to this puddle of water, please."

Destynee tugged her skirt down and did as she was told. Without saying a word, the girl holding the camera began snapping, moving from one side to the other, kneeling down, and then standing back up again. No one talked, the clicking of the camera seemed unusually loud.

"Move your right leg out and point your toe to the far wall. Hold your guitar by the neck."

Lucius had her stand next to a pillar, lean against one side of the pillar, sit on the cement floor, and walk to the far end of the warehouse, turn around, and walk back. The clicks of the camera continued in the silence of the cavernous warehouse. For once, her mother kept quiet as well, which was even stranger.

"Now go to the stairs and sit down, one leg stretched in front and the other leg on a step. Unbutton the top two buttons of your blouse. And turn your body sideways but keep your face towards the camera."

She looked at her mother with a gasp, and then at Lucius. Julee Rae kept silent but gave her a nod.

"It's not that low. I promise. You're still decent." Lucius gave her a nod, too, while the others rolled their eyes and appeared bored.

Destynee looked down at the front of her shirt, and he was right. It wasn't that low plus the rows of ruffles added coverage. She did as she was told.

"Now, go change." Lucius said and then he turned his back on Destynee to consult with the photographer. The other assistants walked closer until they formed a tight circle of whispers and murmurs. Destynee had never felt so self-conscious in her life.

The next ensemble consisted of flared jeans, a

sparkling belt, denim shirt, and a straw cowboy hat. More of the same. Her favorite outfit was the last one. A red dress with a full, flowing skirt that twirled around her black boots.

"Can you have her move?" The photographer lady finally spoke, but she looked directly at Lucius and did not speak to Destynee.

"Sure. Sugar, can you twirl around some? Maybe jump, bringing both feet under you. Great! Now spin again, and walk away from us. Now come back this way. Perfect!" Lucius clapped his hands. "Spin around again."

"Can I keep this dress?" she asked, instead of protesting being called Sugar. That would be a battle for another day.

"Yes, you paid for them," he replied.

"What happens next?" Julee Rae asked.

"We will use these photos to create some ads and posts, and we'll get the word out. I'll need your schedule for the next few weeks so we can advertise you." Lucius walked closer to Destynee and offered his hand, which she shook. "You are a very beautiful girl, Destynee. It's been fun working with you. Be prepared to be recognized, because once these photos get out, you'll be on your way to fame."

She gave him a bright smile, but deep down she was worried. The assistants gathered up the clothes and carried them to the car. Instead of opening the backseat door for them, her mother opened the trunk. "You can toss them back here."

Her mother was unusually quiet on the drive back to the motel.

"Did you think that went okay? I'm anxious to see the photos."

"Those are going to turn out really nice, I think," Julee Rae murmured, a slight frown on her face.

"Thanks, Mom, but what's wrong?"

"Nothing. Nothing at all." Her mother shook her head and gripped the steering wheel. "I can tell you those clothes will not do for any shows you have coming up. You might as well pack them away in a box and keep them in the trunk of the car, or donate them, because they don't suit you at all. I've been buying your costumes since you were four years old. I know what looks good on you and what doesn't."

"Okay, Mom. If it means that much to you, I won't wear them again." Destynee sensed there was something much deeper at issue with her mother, but she didn't really want to keep digging. She had no reason to distrust Lucius, but she couldn't shake the sense of dread that was descending upon her.

25
TRAVIS

"I'M GOING," SKIP ANNOUNCED AS HE APPEARED in the family room wearing a wool jacket, silky red wild rag around his neck, cowboy hat, and hide gloves. "My handsome cowboy." Grace patted his chest. "I think you should get some rest. Besides, it's too cold outside."

"I've rested enough," he protested. "You can't keep babying me, Grace."

"We're not going to be gone that long. Just enough to show Wyatt the lights and decorations and the donkey again." Travis tried to defend his dad, despite the aggravated glance his mother cast in his direction.

"Eeyore!" the little boy lit up.

"Yeah, buddy, we're gonna go see Eeyore."

"May ahh ma!" Wyatt shouted.

"What'd you say, buddy?" Travis looked at Wyatt on his hip.

"I think he means the manger." Skip looked guilty. "We've been going over the story."

Angie came down the stairs. "I'm ready, too."

"Ahhh ma!" Wyatt shouted again.

"Let's go, Travis," his mother said.

"What's he yelling?" asked Angie.

"We have no idea. He has his own little language sometimes." Travis shrugged.

As they pulled closer to the Wild Cow Ranch headquarters, Travis had to drive through several rows of cars to find a spot. They piled out and walked through the grass. Wyatt let out a high-pitched squeal that nearly broke Travis's eardrum. "May ahh ma!"

Travis cupped his ear and looked down at his son. "Take it easy, buddy. We know you're excited."

At dusk the Wild Cow Ranch appeared to be transformed. Festive Christmas lights hung from every fence and structure. White was the predominant color, but the front porches were outlined in red and green and the Nativity was outlined in blue. Garlands were draped on porch railings and buildings. Giant lighted round globes hung from the evergreen trees. Meteor shower rain lights draped over branches of the elms and cottonwoods. Two oversized nutcrackers stood on either side of the entrance into the cookhouse. Buck and Lank had added even more decorations after Travis had left earlier.

The sky was a dusky gray just before the light of the sun completely disappeared and the air felt moist, with a faint glimpse of tiny snowflakes. The headquarters was enchanting, like the inside of a perfect snow globe.

"He's only a kid once." Grace touched her son's arm.

Travis realized that more than she knew, but he couldn't share with his mother how it pierced his heart. *Lord, help me to force that out of my brain. Let me focus on something else.*

"Come on, buddy. Let's go find Eeyore."

People milled around, holding cookies and cups of steaming liquid, and the cold weather didn't seem to bother them one bit. Everyone in the small town knew the Olsens from the Rafter O and hellos were exchanged. Volunteers carried platters piled high with more cookies. The supply seemed endless with all shapes and sizes and flavors.

Ranch foreman Buck spotted them right off and waved. "Hey, there! Glad y'all could make it. Thanks for your help this morning, Travis, on the Nativity shed. It looks good."

"Everything is amazing," said Angie. "I'm going inside to find Carli."

"May ahhh ma!" Wyatt shouted.

"Yeah, little man," Buck said. "Your buddy is over there. He's looking forward to seeing you, too."

"We may be in for a bit of weather, but everyone seems to be bundled up. Lank is supposed to be lighting the bonfire soon." Buck lowered his voice to almost a whisper. "And these people are scoffing up those cookies like crazy. Hope we don't run out."

"Let's get Wyatt over to the petting zoo," said Travis. "That's what we came for."

He led the way, holding Wyatt's hand as Skip and Grace followed.

Wyatt got so excited, he bounced up and down, which would have been a jump, if his legs had been stronger.

"May ahh ma!" He squealed.

Travis and Grace turned to look at each other, saying in unison, "Mayola, the llama."

"That's what he's been trying to say all day." Travis chuckled as he reached for the latch on the gate. "Well come on then, and let's go see that llama. You wouldn't pet him this morning."

Kaylee the babysitter walked into the corral, working her way through the sheep and goats, towards Wyatt. Travis picked Wyatt up so he could see Mayola closer.

"It's okay. You can pet him," said Kaylee. "See." She rubbed her hand along the animal's neck and then backed away a little. "As long as he doesn't spit at me."

Wyatt reached out chubby fingers and patted the neck, too.

"He is adorable. I'm taking pictures. Look this way, Wyatt," said Kaylee.

"Yes, my nephew is a cutie pie," Angie said. "I'm taking pictures, too."

Between the two of them, they photographed Wyatt petting everything that he could get his hands on. Once he got brave enough to approach the animals, they couldn't stop him. Travis never realized how entertaining a toddler could be. Despite the ache of wishing for Destynee to be there with them, he still laughed at his precocious son.

"I don't think it's necessary that he pet every sheep, Mother." Travis stood with his arms folded across his chest watching Grace tail Wyatt around the pen.

"But he wants to," Grace said.

"Would you send me those pictures?" asked Angie. "I'd like to post them on my social."

"Sure thing," said Kaylee. She turned to Travis. "And speaking of social, your wife's photographs are gorgeous. She is everywhere and really building up her followers. I've watched every video she's posted. What an amazing voice she has."

Travis half listened to the babysitter gushing about his wife, and then he realized he had no idea what she was talking about. He looked at her, trying to register what she was saying.

"I went to her website to buy tickets, but some of her shows this next week are already sold out. Can you believe it?"

"Sold out?" Travis was still blank. A zillion questions ran through his mind. Rather than broaching the subject, he decided to divert everyone's attention elsewhere. "Let's go look at the Nativity and get a cookie."

"I'll see y'all next week," said Kaylee.

Skip smiled and headed towards the cookie table. His wife called after him. "Skip Olsen, you just take one."

Angie scooped up Wyatt which started a few whining protests, but she tickled his tummy and said, "Cookie!" Pretty soon he forgot what he was upset about. Grace and Travis brought up the rear as they walked back towards the cookhouse.

The living Nativity was lovely with costumed volunteers dressed in traditional clothing. Travis was happy to see that the donkey named Eeyore stood perfectly still in his spot and knew Wyatt would start squealing again when he saw him.

A solemn and devout looking Joseph suddenly raised a hand and waved. "Howdy, Travis. Hey there, Olsen family!"

Travis threw his head back and let out a choking laugh. "You'd better stay in character, Wilson."

"Hey, can you bring me a cookie? I'm starving." Wilson turned his smile into a pout and put his hands together in a prayer.

"We can do that for you," said Angie. "Don't worry. We wouldn't let 'Joseph' starve." She chuckled.

Wyatt was more than a little excited about seeing the

donkey again and he did get a lot of petting in. But soon his smile turned into a red face and he started coughing.

"Maybe he's had enough. Let's get him inside the house," Grace said.

Travis carried him and they headed to Lola and Buck's apartment.

Inside they removed his jacket and tried to settle him down. Wyatt started crying a little and Travis saw that his face was flushed. In a weak voice, he managed to mutter, "Mama."

It broke Travis's heart.

And just like always Travis felt frustration over being unable to explain to the toddler why his mother wasn't here. For days, months now, he'd been forgiving her and allowing her the benefit of the doubt. She has a gift. She must be busy. She'd be home soon. How long could he keep saying those things?

But now he was angry. Angry at himself. Angry at her. What in the world was she thinking? Was her career more important than her baby boy? And why didn't she call them?

Return his voicemails? What was really going on with her?

"Grace, I've got a thermometer. Let's take his temperature." Lola's face was serious.

Little Wyatt's eyes drooped and he was becoming more lethargic. But also coughing more, and then he gave his grandma a little smile as if nothing was wrong.

Lola read the thermometer. "It's not too high. Just a smidge."

"Thanks, Lola." And then to Travis, she said, "I think he's more tired than anything."

"He's not the only one," said Skip.

"Give our thanks to Carli and Lank. It was a wonderful Open House this year."

"I wish y'all could stay. We're about to sing Christmas carols around the bonfire. We've got plenty of hot cocoa and coffee. I'm sorry little Wyatt is not feeling well."

"Oh, he's okay, I'm sure. He had a long day," said Grace.

Travis was thankful that everyone was ready to go. He was in no mood to sing or eat a cookie or look at any more decorations without his entire family with him. His arm hung useless without his wife's shoulders to rest it on. There was an emptiness everywhere he went. The missing piece would always be Destynee.

He just had to figure out a way to convince her of where she belonged. There had to be a way that they both could get what they wanted.

26
TRAVIS

THE COUGHING WOULD NOT STOP. WYATT HAD coughed so much his little body was exhausted, and it had turned into a cough between sobs, with big tears rolling down his cheeks. He was mad, too.

Travis sat on one edge of the toddler bed arranging pillows to prop Wyatt up so he could breathe. He had cried so much, now his nose was stopped up. That made him mad, too. The crying turned into screaming.

Grace turned on the light and went closer to Wyatt's bed and picked him up.

"He's really warm. I'm going to take his temperature."

Travis moved to help her. "Here, I'll hold him while you do that." Wyatt was fidgety and whining. Travis tried to encourage him. "It's okay, buddy."

She read the thermometer. "It's one-oh-one. We should go to the emergency room. I'm giving him some baby Tylenol first. That should make him feel better."

"Let me get dressed and I'll meet you outside. What about Dad?"

"I'll tell him we're going. He should be all right for a few hours. I'll call Angie soon to look in on him."

Travis got dressed first and then he wrapped Wyatt in a blanket, tossed some extra diapers in a bag, and rushed out the door. When Travis brought Wyatt outside, his folks were standing near his truck.

"Dad. What're you doin' out of bed? It's after two in the morning."

"If my little buddy is sick, I'm goin' with him."

Grace looked at Travis and shrugged. "There was no stopping him."

TRAVIS DROVE AS FAST as he dared on the dirt roads, and when he hit the blacktop, he opened it up. There wouldn't be any traffic this late at night. He had to back off of his speed when he noticed the empty roads were slick and the weather was changing to a wintery mix. Great, just what they needed.

His father was in the passenger seat and his mother was in the back rubbing Wyatt's leg who was fidgeting and crying in his car seat.

"It's okay, baby. We're almost there. The doctors will help you to feel better."

Travis was grateful for his parents' constant presence in his and Wyatt's life. And right now they all had to concentrate on his son's well-being.

Once inside the Emergency Room of the Amarillo hospital personnel presented Travis with forms to complete while Grace held Wyatt who was worn out and drifting from near-sleep to all out wailing.

Finally, a nurse led them to an exam room and took down the history. What were the symptoms, when did they first start, was he a preemie at birth, how were his urine and bowel output...tons of questions. Another nurse took his vitals and said to the first nurse, "Temp is one-oh-two."

Grace said, "It was one-oh-one at home."

The nurses disrobed Wyatt down to his diaper and Travis watched his little chest heave up and down, struggling for breaths.

A woman in a white coat, with a stethoscope around her neck, came into the room. "Hello. I'm Doctor Mercedez." She held the digital chart and read as she walked to the side of the bed.

"So has Wyatt had this cough and cold for a while?" She looked at Travis and Grace as she placed a hand on Wyatt's chest.

Grace answered first. "Not really. Well, kind of off and on. You know, normal kid sniffles here and there. It was just the other day we noticed a cough."

"And then earlier," Travis said. "He didn't stop coughing."

"I'd like to do a couple of tests to make sure. It could be RSV. First, I'd like to get him on oxygen to help with his breathing. We might need to put him in an oxygen tent."

She nodded to the nurse who readied the equipment. "He might fuss at that so we'll give him something mild to settle him down."

"What is RSV?" Travis asked.

"Respiratory syncytial virus. It's actually quite common in young children. Most of them get it from being around other kids, runny noses, touching each other, transferring germs. Sometimes germs on surfaces. Day care centers can run rampant with RSV."

"Wyatt doesn't go to a day care."

"Has he been around another child lately who sees other children? Or maybe an older person with a compromised system? With an illness?"

Grace and Travis looked at each other stunned.

"Gabriel?"

"Skip?"

Grace explained. "Gabriel is my other grandson. The two boys played a few days back. But Gabriel didn't appear sick." She then touched Skip's arm. And my husband was in the hospital recently in a coma from a horse accident. But he hasn't had a cold and I'm always disinfecting my kitchen counter and other surfaces. And the kids' toys, too."

The doctor smiled with an understanding look. "My bet would be the other grandson. Especially if he's exposed to other kids. But we can't be sure where they pick it up from. You also told the nurse he went to an Open House. Being around a lot of people and other kids can add to a lower immune system."

Travis asked, "Will you give him antibiotics?"

"No. Usually the virus ignores antibiotics. We might have to just let it run its course. Usually, eight to ten days. We'll keep an eye on him. Give him oxygen and fluids."

"You'll keep him in the hospital that long?" Travis was starting to panic.

"Just for a few days probably. When he's stable, you can take him home. Let me run those tests to confirm that it is RSV. The nurse will start an I.V. to get fluids into him. And don't worry. We have new technology that delivers numbing medication first so that the needle doesn't hurt at all. Soon he'll feel a little drowsy so he won't fight the oxygen tube in his nose. And then we'll get the tent up if need be."

They thanked the doctor as she left the ER cubicle and watched all of the procedures the nurses carried out.

Travis thought his bloodshot eyes must've looked like a deer in the headlights. This whole thing was scary. He loved this little guy with his whole being and hated to watch him in any kind of pain or discomfort. All kinds of freak things could happen. What if Wyatt just stopped breathing? Or if his temperature kept rising? He'd seen television programs about babies dying in hospitals. Dear God, please protect my son.

His stomach churned and he felt sick. He needed to call Destynee, and if she wouldn't answer he would call Julee Rae. Wyatt needed his mother to be here with him.

"I'll be back in a minute, Mom."

He walked down the hall and saw an Exit sign and pushed the outer door open. Outside in the winter mist he took a gulp of the cold air. Please help us, Lord. Protect Wyatt. Don't take my son.

As soft as his heart was at this moment and filled with fatherly love, he also felt white-hot anger rising up in him, gaining steam. He wasn't used to it and it almost felt evil but he couldn't shake it away.

Where was his wife? Didn't she love them anymore? Had she left them? Maybe he didn't really know her after all. Was she that selfish?

He made up his mind. He would not call her again, would not try to force her to want to be in their lives. That was entirely her choice now. The idea suddenly struck him that he could do this on his own, without Destynee by his side. He would raise Wyatt and be the best father that he could be. A sudden peace washed over him along with the realization that Wyatt was going to be all right.

Thank you, Lord.

27
TRAVIS

QUIETLY ENTERING THE ROOM, HE SAW HIS mother with head bowed, his father was sitting in the vinyl recliner with eyes closed, both obviously praying for Wyatt. She looked up.

"You okay, Travis?"

"Yeah, Mom. I'm okay. Just needed some air."

"It's hard, I know. Your father and I went through this with five kids. Cuts, scrapes, broken bones, appendicitis."

"Lots of vomit and blood," Skip added.

She half-smiled, then frowned.

Travis smiled slightly and shook his head. "Yeah, I guess you must've gone through a lot with our crazy crew."

"But you know what, Travis? I wouldn't have traded one minute of all that anguish for the alternative—not having you kids in our lives. Y'all have been a tremendous blessing for us."

"It's so scary though. I don't know how y'all got through it."

"We prayed and we held onto each other."

Their conversation was interrupted by a nurse entering the room.

"I'm here to check his vitals. We're still running a couple of tests and the doctor will be in soon to talk with you," she said.

"Thank you." Travis gritted his teeth to stay strong when he really felt like letting the tears flow. He bent forward in the chair and looked to the floor at his boots.

"Aren't you Diane's daughter? I'm Grace Olsen. I know your mom through the Chamber toy drive."

The nurse lingered, chart in hand, and then she turned to Grace with a surprised look on her face. "Yes, I am. I remember now. I graduated with your daughter, Janie."

"I never knew you went to school to be a nurse."

"Yes, I did. Tried a teaching degree first, but realized this is what I really wanted to do." She turned to Travis. "And you're married to Destynee now. I think it's great that she's following her dream."

Travis looked up, his brow crinkled. "What?"

"I love her singing. She is so talented. You must be very proud. I've watched all of her videos."

He was puzzled. Another person who mentioned videos. He never knew that Destynee had ever been recorded singing. Must be Julee Rae's doings.

"She's really getting famous. I love her singing." The young nurse giggled. "I said that already. I follow her on social media and am planning to go with my friends to her next concert. I'm honored to be taking care of her son. And don't worry. I won't take any pictures of him. I could lose my job if I did that. And it wouldn't be right anyway."

Now he was truly confused.

"Famous? What are you talking about? Social media?"

"Yes. Her career is skyrocketing. People love her. She has such an angelic voice. And she's so pretty. Seems genuine, too. Down to earth."

"What did you say about social media? Where is her next concert?"

"Haven't you seen it yet? Here, let me get my phone. I'll show you."

The nurse pulled her phone from her pocket and clicked on one of her social media accounts and handed the phone to Travis.

He was startled to see his wife's painted face, curled hair, and most of all, her plunging neckline in a glittering red dress. This didn't look like the Destynee he knew. She was so different.

He tapped the screen and his wife's sweet voice filled the room.

Grace looked up. "Is that Destynee?"

Travis nodded.

That venom again filled his head. He had to look away. She was becoming a total stranger to him.

"Thank you," he said to the nurse and handed her phone back.

"Hope I didn't say anything wrong," she said.

"No, you're fine."

As the nurse left the room, he looked at his mother and father, shook his head, then lowered it. "I don't even know her anymore. It's obvious she doesn't want to be in our lives."

"Oh, Travis. Try calling her. She needs to know about Wyatt."

"No!" he snapped. "Do you know how many messages I've left her? She just ignores them. That's it. I am *not* calling her again. And I don't want anyone else calling her. What's the point?"

His mother's voice was very quiet. "Travis, there must be something going on that we don't know about. A misunderstanding. Maybe she lost her phone. I've been praying for both of you."

"Mom, I don't even know if that helps anymore."

"Please don't give up, Travis. Let's just focus on the most important thing in our lives at the moment. Little Wyatt. He needs us."

Travis just nodded and kept his head lowered to his lap.

Doctor Mercedez entered the exam room with a smile.

"Wyatt does have RSV but he's a strong little boy. I want to admit him for a couple of days. When it is time for him to go home, lots of rest and fluids. Don't let him get too excited. Keep him away from other children who may have compromised systems, a cold or cough. In other words, germy." She smiled again and put her hand on Wyatt's chest as he peacefully slept.

"What about antibiotics?" Travis asked.

"No. Not for RSV, which is a virus not a bacteria. For high-risk children, like preemies or ones with a heart condition, there is an antibody. But not for a healthy child like Wyatt."

"Will he need oxygen at home? Or an inhaler?" Grace asked.

"No. Just keep an eye on him. If he starts wheezing drastically like he's in trouble, bring him back to the ER. But usually, this gets better on its own. There are no vaccines, no instant cure. It just takes time."

Grace smiled. "Thank you, Doctor."

"Yes, thank you." Travis stroked his son's tiny arm.

"Let him sleep. The oxygen and fluids are helping. And his temp should start coming down soon."

The doctor left them and Grace bowed her head and clasped her hands. "Thank you, God, for protecting our little Wyatt."

Travis noticed the moisture on his mother's face, and he wished he could make her feel better. This was out of his power now.

"Mom, you and Dad go on home. Get some rest. I'm staying here tonight."

"Are you sure? We can get a motel close by."

"No. You'll sleep better in your own bed. Dad needs to take care of his health, too. Here's my keys. Take my truck."

"Okay, if you're sure. Can we get you anything? Something to drink? A snack?"

"Oh, I could use some one-dollar bills for the vending machine. I'll get me something later." He kissed his mom's cheek and hugged his dad. "Goodnight. Thank you."

"We'll be back early in the morning," Grace said.

And she meant it, too. Probably before the sun rose. Grace wouldn't stay away long. After they'd left, Travis squinted to see through the clear plastic oxygen tent they had set up for his son. He was sleeping peacefully. Travis sat back in the recliner and pulled the foot rest out. It wasn't as soft as the easy chairs in his mother's den, but it would do. It felt good to finally sit down.

He pulled his phone out of his pocket, made sure it was on silent, and tapped the internet. He noticed he didn't have many bars in the room. The only thing he used his phone for was to check the weather and the cattle prices. Other than that, he rarely surfed the web. It was foreign to him, and he couldn't understand how people spent hours of their time staring at their phones.

In the search bar he typed 'Destynee', and the first site that popped up was Destynee dot com. He was surprised, to say the least.

He barely recognized his wife. Wild, curly hair and a mini skirt, a saucy look on her face. She set his pulses racing alright, but she probably did that for a million other guys if they happened to look at this website. He couldn't take his eyes off her and he couldn't stop looking at the pictures.

It looked like she was in an abandoned warehouse, and he had to admit he liked the edgy look versus the glittery dresses her mother usually had her wear. This was a different Destynee. More confident, more worldly. He followed the links to other sites, but most of them he had never heard of, and he didn't want to take the time to set up an account. He could do that later. He went back to the search page and noticed videos of her singing. He'd have to look at those later, too.

The tour dates page was still under construction. One thing was for certain, Destynee was moving on and leaving them all behind.

28
DESTYNEE

14 DAYS TO CHRISTMAS

THE VENUE WAS AN OLD THEATER IN ABILENE. Her mother parked the car, and Destynee grabbed her bag and guitar case. They had driven around and around, finally finding a parking space on the front side of the building instead of near the stage entrance.

For tonight's performance, her mother had insisted on a tight, red sequin gown that didn't feel right. That red flowy dress and black boots she had worn for the photo shoot stayed in her thoughts, but she was afraid to say anything, much less put it on. She liked everything to run smoothly, no confrontations, no stress, which is why she did what her mother wanted. Life was so much easier when Julee Rae got her way. Destynee used to not mind following her mother's instructions, but now it all seemed wrong. Her clothes. This place. Even her singing.

Without waiting for her mother, Destynee took off towards the theater which looked like it was a mile away on the far side of a sea of parked vehicles. She sighed. The opportunity to sing used to make her giddy with excitement, but now she had lost the joy and it made her sad.

Stepping inside, she was taken by surprise. With gold velvet drapes on the stage and worn wooden seats covered in red velvet, it would be one of the largest audiences she had played for this season. She paused at the back, not so much from nerves but to admire the elaborate decoration and wonder about all the acts that had performed on that very stage. She couldn't deny the thrill knowing she would be standing on it later that evening. The intricate carved wood work that arched over the stage area glistened from the massive chandelier that hung in the center of the ceiling. It looked as though almost every seat was full.

She had been asked to participate in a holiday show, which her mother had booked months ago, and she had been working on nothing else but "Rockin' Around the Christmas Tree" for the past three days, made popular by Brenda Lee. Destynee sometimes felt that she'd been born in the wrong decade. She loved the old songs.

"You're Destynee!" A young woman stepped close and gave her a hug despite the fact that it wasn't returned. "I just love your voice."

Several other people gathered around her.

"We came to see you." A young family, two young boys, and their parents beamed at her.

"What are you singing tonight?"

She searched past the small crowd that had formed, but didn't see her mother. "Excuse me, please. I have to get backstage."

More people gathered around.

"We loved your website," an older lady grabbed her

arm. "My granddaughter and I have watched all your videos."

Videos? Website?

A man pushed his way through the crowd. "Move aside, folks. Give her some air. Follow me." He caught her eye and took her guitar case with one hand. With the other he grabbed her arm and pulled her through the mass of people. "Excuse us. Let us pass, please. She needs to get ready for the show."

When they were clear of the crowd, Destynee took a deep breath. "Thank you."

"What were you thinking coming in the front door with the audience?" He stopped and narrowed his eyes at her. "That was the stupidest thing I've ever seen. Didn't you get my email with the passcode for the door? I gave you explicit instructions on where to go."

"No, no—sorry."

"If only you artists would follow my direction you would make my job so much easier. I don't understand why you people can't read an email." He tugged her up the stage stairs, and around to the backstage area which buzzed with people and the occasional musical instrument, suddenly stopping at a door. "This is you. And why weren't you here for rehearsals? Normally you would be nixed, but some of our locals remember you from last year. You're lucky to have so much talent otherwise you'd be out on your ear, that's for sure."

With one shove she was in the room and then the door slammed shut in her face. She had never been treated that way before. She turned to sit on the stool that faced a small counter and lighted mirror. The door swung open and her mother walked in, collapsing in the faded leather chair in the corner, the only other piece of furniture in the room.

"Mother. Did you know anything about a rehearsal that I missed?" Destynee spun around to face her.

"Oh, yes. We got an email. You don't need to rehearse. You'll do just fine." Julee Rae walked up behind Destynee. "Sit still while I do something with that hair."

From a satchel, she pulled out a brush and box of hairpins. Pulling the hair into a tight ponytail that made Destynee's scalp tingle, her mother then fashioned it into a bun.

"It's not a matter of whether I can sing or not, it's a matter of having a sound check, meeting the lighting crew, and being involved in the production. I'm not sure what order the acts are. When do I go on?" Destynee stood to pace back and forth.

"There's no sense in getting upset over this. It's really not that big a deal." Julee Rae pulled a lipstick from her purse and moved to the stool in front of the mirror. While she concentrated on her face Destynee paced some more, although the room was only big enough for a few steps back and a few steps in the other direction. She finally sunk into the leather chair, because her mother could take next to an hour touching up her own makeup before Destynee would get a turn.

Her phone showed no texts, no missed calls. In her state of mind, that was one more thing added to a long list of annoyances that made her mad. You would think her husband would have the courtesy to at least let her know how Skip was doing. She wanted to be kept in the loop and be involved with her in-laws' lives, but Travis was making that impossible. Shutting her out. He was only isolating her further from them.

The only consolation was that he and Wyatt were probably getting ready for bed by now. She imagined them in her old room, Travis reading a book to Wyatt as he snuggled under the covers. She sighed. And then she heard thunderous applause. The show was starting. Opening her dressing room door, she walked softly towards the stage area until she could see the Master of Ceremonies welcoming everyone. He reviewed the acts, which included a local girl who had gone big in Nashville, Stella May. Destynee remembered her from last year.

Something hit her shoulder, and she stumbled to one side losing her balance. Destynee turned to apologize.

"You can't stand here." It was Stella May herself, her eyes raking Destynee from head to toe with a disapproving glance. Another small-town girl who had gotten a big break and someone who Destynee admired greatly. She had followed her meteoric rise on the country music charts.

It was her confidence and her arrogance, not to mention the fact that her appearance was flawless. Not one blonde hair out of place. Even the fringe on her skirt seemed to sway in perfect unison. The scowl turned to a brilliant smile as she turned to face the audience. They exploded with applause. Stepping up to the microphone, the girl gave the MC a hug, turned, and belted the opening lines of "Rockin' Around the Christmas Tree." And it was very good. She killed it.

Destynee's heart dropped to her knees. She stumbled back into her dressing room and shut the door.

"What's wrong? Are you about to throw up?" Julee Rae gave her a look of utter disgust.

Before Destynee could reply, a tap on the door followed by "Five minutes."

Without another glance towards her mother, she walked to the mirror, checked her face, grabbed her guitar, and took a spot in the wings. Her heart pounded so hard, it made her breathless. She closed her eyes and willed herself to focus on her breathing. Blocked thoughts about the ridiculous sequins that covered her body. The son and husband who lived their life without her. Instead, she thought about the song she wanted to sing. She fixated in her head on her fingers strumming the notes. And when they announced her name, she walked on stage emulating the same confidence and arrogance as Stella May. Because Destynee could sing the heck out of any song, too.

The notes from her guitar floated through the theater as the audience quieted. Her voice was soft and angelic, the first line almost a whisper. "Mary Did You Know?" and the place grew silent and still as her voice floated over their heads. They were spellbound.

She knew it was one of the best performances of her career.

29
DESTYNEE

DESTYNEE WALKED OFF STAGE ON A HIGH, AND with a sense of peace and a confidence she had rarely felt these past few months. She loved singing religious music, and "Mary Did You Know?" was one of her all-time favorites. She never imagined that an opportunity would come along that would enable her to sing it in front of such a large audience.

The man who had been so rude before and had saved her from the crowd earlier now stood with mouth agape blocking her path. "That was amazing."

She gave him a shy smile. "Thank you. The acoustics are out of this world."

"My name is Blaise and yes, this old building has witnessed some amazing performances. It is such an honor to hear you sing. The audience was mesmerized by you. I've never seen anything like it."

"Glad to meet you, Blaise. How many people are here, would you guess?"

"It was a sellout crowd. This old theater actually seats around two thousand."

Two thousand people? Destynee had no idea there were that many.

"Be prepared. You will be bombarded with autograph seekers after the show. Don't go anywhere, because after that performance the producers may ask you to squeeze in another song, and then we want you on stage for the finale. They're singing 'We Wish You a Merry Christmas.' Let me know if you need anything."

That was a first. She had been moved around on the playbill many times for one reason or another in the past, but never added. Usually canceled. As she walked into her dressing room, her mother was going through an oversized suitcase of costumes.

"Hurry and change. The producer of the show stopped by. They want you to sing again." She held up a hunter green glittering nightmare with fringe and a gaudy jeweled band around the neck. "This will work."

"Mother." Destynee spoke louder than she intended, but it got Julee Rae's attention. "I'm wearing that red dress from the photo shoot. It suits me better, I think. None of the other acts are wearing sequined gowns and I feel overdressed."

She walked over to the suitcase and dug to the very bottom where she had hidden it, and pulled it out along with her boots, too. In her makeup carryall, she searched in the side pocket for silver hoop earrings that Travis had given her their first Christmas together. And her guitar. That's all she needed. Now she had to think about song choices and do something about that dress. Poking her head out the door, she caught the attention of a young man with a clipboard. "Can you send Blaise to my dressing room, please?"

"Yes, ma'am. Right away, ma'am."

She had to giggle at his nervousness. Giving a

knockout performance had its rewards. Within minutes there was a tap on the door. It swung open, and Blaise asked, "What can I help you with?"

"I'd like to know what the other artists are singing. I'm trying to decide what to do for my second song. Is it traditional Christmas songs or more gospel selections?"

He opened his cell phone and showed her the list. She studied it for a few minutes.

"Great. That's what I needed to know. Thank you. And I have one more favor."

"Just name it," Blaise said.

"I need an iron in the worst way." She held up the wrinkled mess of a dress.

"Oh my, yes you do. Let me have it." He snatched it out of her hand, slamming the door shut behind him.

"What are you singing?" Julee Rae asked. "Don't embarrass me. I have worked too hard to get us here."

"I haven't decided yet."

"Well, you need to decide quick. How about 'Jolly Old St. Nicholas'? Something fun and cheery. That first song you sang was too slow and not appropriate for this production. Why did you change from what you had rehearsed?" Julee Rae continued to sort through the pile of dresses. She held up a bright purple floor-length gown with a jeweled bodice. Destynee frowned and shook her head no.

"Because the other singer sang the song I was going to sing, Mother. Didn't you hear her?"

"Oh. I didn't listen." With an overly exasperated gesture she began folding the clothes and stacking them back inside the suitcase.

"Did you listen to my song?"

Her mother hesitated as if choosing her words carefully, before she responded. "I heard the first part, and then realized it wasn't the song you had been rehearsing. And then I felt a headache coming on so I went outside to get some fresh air."

That last comment stung. The people she cared about the most had missed her singing. A performance that in her mind might very well be the turning point of her career. She felt that things were about to change, but she couldn't point to any specifics. She had the sense that a new door had opened and that she would have to decide whether to step through it or not.

Blaise suddenly appeared in her dressing room holding the red dress neatly pressed on a hanger. "Here ya go. Knock 'em dead." He smiled and winked. "You're on in ten."

Destynee waited until the door was shut, and then hurriedly stepped out of the gown she wore. Within seconds she was ready. She touched up her face, pulled a few strands from the sides of her hair with a clippie leaving the rest long to hang down her back, and slid her feet into the boots. She felt like a small-town girl with her guitar singing the songs she loved. That's who she was.

Her mother watched from the easy chair, not saying a word or offering criticism, which was highly unusual. Maybe Julee Rae felt a change in the air, too. Whatever was the reason, she certainly wasn't happy. A deep frown made the wrinkles on her forehead more prominent.

She considered what her mother had said about a song that would be cheerful and fun for the audience. Not a bad idea to get everyone in the holiday spirit. But all the other acts had done just that. Traditional holiday tunes, lively and upbeat. It had been a fun evening. If she wanted to stand out and be remembered, she needed to do the exact opposite. The producers hadn't asked what she intended to sing, which she interpreted as she had free rein to decide.

A tap on the door signaled it was time. Destynee reapplied lipstick and left without saying a word to her mother. Before she walked on stage for the second time, the musical director asked if she needed any musicians to accompany her. As professionals, they probably knew every song she knew.

"I've got my guitar. That's all I need but thank you."

Blaise appeared at her side. "Lights?"

"Dim with one spotlight on me, please," she said.

"You got it."

"Put your hands together one more time for Destynee!" The emcee turned and stretched out an arm in her direction, giving her a wide smile that was all white teeth under a stiff, perfectly coiffed head of hair. She walked to the spot behind the microphone, the red cotton dress swirling around black boots.

She waited for the applause to die down. "Hi, I'm Destynee from Dixon and I'd like to sing y'all another song." She strummed the familiar opening notes and began the sorrowful words, "I'll be Home for Christmas."

Images of her son Wyatt and Travis floated through her mind as she sang, and the sadness of missing them came through her voice. She couldn't have sounded unhappier if she had tried. And when she sang the line about it being only in her dreams, she was helpless to stop the tear that rolled down her check.

She couldn't see the audience because of the bright spotlight, so she pretended that she was singing directly to Travis. Telling him that she wanted to be with him more than any place in the world. She sang to that dark void and gave it everything she had.

As the final notes of her guitar faded, the stage lights popped on and the house lights came up, and the audience erupted with applause. Within seconds they were on their feet, and she noticed a few people on the front rows had damp faces and were wiping their eyes.

She bowed low and walked off stage to see that the people standing in the wings were also applauding. Her mother was nowhere in sight. And neither were the two faces she had sung to, for that matter.

30
DESTYNEE

14 DAYS UNTIL CHRISTMAS

"ENCORE. ENCORE!"

"Listen to that. They want you back." Blaise pointed to the audience as Destynee stood in the wings backstage hardly believing her ears. The emcee leaned close listening to a man wearing jeans and a dark sports jacket who exuded confidence as the one in charge. The emcee nodded his head and hurried back onstage.

"We'll have Destynee back again, but in the meantime let's hear from our hometown girl, Stella May."

The man walked over to her. "Well, what do you say? Do you have another one in you?"

"Yes sir, I believe I do."

"Great. Stay right there and we'll send you out in a few minutes. You have done an exceptional job for us."

"Anything in particular you'd like me to sing?"

"Completely up to you. You are so talented, and we really appreciate your being here." He gave her a warm smile and a pat on the back. “You’re going to have an amazing career, young lady, if you keep working hard.”

Destynee could only nod because her stomach was doing flips as she thought about song choices. What now? She never imagined an opportunity like this. She had less than a few minutes to decide. She wanted to call Travis and ask him. He would know what to do.

The headliner finished, took a bow and walked towards Destynee, the smile she had given to the audience suddenly replaced by hatred-filled eyes. As Stella May walked past, she murmured through gritted teeth so only Destynee could hear, “That was supposed to be my encore.”

Shaking off the comment, a thousand song lyrics swirled in her head. And then she thought about all her favorites and the songs that meant so much to her. She couldn’t choose.

“I’d like to do two more songs for you, if that’s okay.” She blurted out before she even thought about the consequences of taking such privilege. Rather than glancing in the wings, she forged ahead.

She could hear the applause swell but she couldn’t see any faces because of the spotlights. She decided to sing “My Favorite Things.” The applause was immediate as soon as she sang the first line, and then quieted. The band behind her joined in and she had never had more fun.

“Thank you! I’d like to slow things down a bit and end with one of my favorites, ‘How Great Thou Art.’”

Her voice seemed to soar to the rafters. She had never sounded better. She took a deep breath and gave it her all on the last verse. The roar of applause surprised her and when the house lights came up, they were on their feet again. Tears swelled in her eyes and pride expanded her heart. This is what she was meant to do. Blessing folks with her voice, touching their lives with God's message. She had spent so much time in bars and at bar-b-ques, she had lost her way. But tonight, she found it again.

The other acts surrounded her on stage and she joined them in singing "We Wish You a Merry Christmas." The curtain dropped and the show was over.

THE CROWD JAMMED into the hall and blocked her dressing room door. She inched her way through them, until someone said her name and that's when all chaos broke loose.

"Can I have your autograph?"

"You are an amazing singer!"

"Would you sign my shirt?"

Thank goodness Blaise suddenly appeared to save her again from the storm. "Give her some air, folks. If y'all would move to the front lobby, I'll make sure Destynee joins you in a few minutes." He opened her dressing room door and ushered her in, closing the door behind her.

"Well, that was something." He laughed.

"Was it all right that I sang two more songs instead of just one?"

Blaise laughed again, this time a deep throated belly laugh. "It was more than all right. You slayed it, Destynee!"

"Now, freshen up your face and calm your nerves, because your fans await. I'll be back in five to escort you to the lobby where all the acts will gather for a meet and greet." He paused before leaving and turned around to meet her eyes. "That's some God-given talent right there. Don't ever stop sharing your gift."

That last bit surprised her and left her speechless. He closed the door behind him leaving Destynee staring at the spot where he had stood. She didn't know how to process that information, but for once in her life she completely understood what he was trying to tell her. It was a God-given talent, but He had also blessed her with a husband and child. How would she ever juggle the two worlds? *Help me, Lord. Just show me the way.*

"WELL, THAT WAS CERTAINLY DIFFERENT." Julee Rae pulled out of the theater parking lot two hours later. She didn't try to hide her annoyance.

Normally Destynee would have stayed backstage out of sight while Julee Rae networked with the people who scouted the talent, until she was ready to leave.

"Isn't this what you wanted, Mother? Fans to recognize me. For some reason they sure did tonight. I've never signed my name so many times in my life."

"I guess we're getting our money's worth from Lucius."

"What do you mean?"

"He made you a website, but I haven't had time to look at it."

Destynee searched on her cell phone for any texts or missed calls from her husband first. If only she could talk to him and tell him about tonight. His opinion was so critical as she decided on the next move for her career. And Christian music was tugging on her heart in a big way.

The search for her name resulted in more information than she thought possible and, sure enough, it came up at the top of the list. Search results also produced several different social media accounts in her name, which she clicked on just to get a first glance. She would go back and read every word and fan comment when they got to the motel.

"He has me everywhere."

"Good. That's what I wanted." Julee Rae pulled into the drive through of a fast-food place. "Are you hungry?"

"Not really. I'm just ready to get in bed."

"I'm starving." While Julee Rae ordered, Destynee kept reading about herself.

The photographs from the warehouse were put to good use, all different and posted on the various sites. The lighting and reflection from the dirty puddle of water were exceptional. She still liked that red dress. It photographed so well. And also gave her a homespun, natural look—so unlike those glittery numbers her mother wanted her to wear.

She clicked on the link to her website and had to admit it wasn't bad. Definitely country and small-town girl vibes with pictures of a pasture and blue bonnets, obvious Texas branding. One page had her upcoming dates listed with towns and events she didn't even know about. She was booked right up until Christmas Eve.

Under the tab marked "Press" she found more photographs and a question-and-answer list. She had never seen any of those questions before in her life, as well as personal information.

"This lists me as currently single. We need to change that."

Julee Rae pulled into the parking lot. "I've already checked us in."

Destynee was surprised to see they had upgraded the hotel accommodations by a lot. "This is a nice place."

"Well, the producers paid you a nice bonus after tonight's performance plus they comped our hotel room."

It wasn't just a nice room; it was a suite with two separate rooms and a living area. She could get used to this she thought as she stepped into one of the bedrooms. A Queen-sized bed with four fluffy pillows in the color scheme of gold and black. A red leather easy chair filled one corner. What a wonderful sight. And the living room was big, too, with a couch, coffee pot, small refrigerator with drinks, and in the center of the coffee table a complimentary fruit basket. She bounced from one thing to the next, delighted at each new discovery, and then suddenly felt hungry. Collapsing on the sofa, she unwrapped the cellophane to get a better view of the choices. Fresh fruit and dried, plus cheese and crackers. It all looked delicious.

Julee Rae ate her greasy burger, the smell of which almost made Destynee gag.

"I'm getting in the shower," her mother said as she disappeared into the second bedroom and shut the door behind her.

"Okay, goodnight." Part of her had hoped to talk to her mother about the night's performance. She felt that it was one of her best, but she would have liked to have heard it from the one person who had been traveling with her on the road these past few months. Mostly she felt drained and yet still on edge. Things were going to change; she just knew it. Change to what she did not know.

Destynee wanted some time alone, too, so that she could read everything on her website without her mother watching over her shoulder. She needed time to think and consider the best path for her career. The epiphany she had during tonight's performance was hard to deny.

Once she heard the shower running, she felt at ease to pull off her boots and settle back, and click the link again. It really was well done. The website depicted a serious artist, which she was, but she had never told the rest of the world that. She clicked the link marked "Press" and then clicked "Photos." What pictures from the photo shoot hadn't been used on the other sites, were grouped together in this section.

She froze. "No."

A chill went down her spine and she felt tears prick the back of her eyes. It was the pose on the stairs with the short skirt and thigh high boots. The angle and the light, her bare thighs, her shirt unbuttoned lower than normal, and the saucy look on her face. She never imagined herself to look that sexy. Definitely not the image of a wife and mother, or of a soon-to-be Christian music singer.

"Travis." His name came from her lips before she even realized she had muttered it aloud. If he saw this, he would be furious as he had every right to be. She didn't care how late it was, she needed to talk to her husband.

31
DESTYNEE

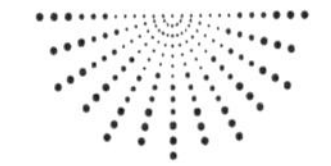

13 DAYS UNTIL CHRISTMAS

DESTYNEE TAPPED THE NUMBERS IN FOR HER mother's landline at their house in Dixon, as if punching harder would make Travis answer and calm her panic.

"Please pick up. Please pick up." She didn't care if the ringing phone woke up Wyatt. She had to talk to her husband.

If she couldn't explain the situation to him on the phone, then she'd show up on his doorstep. He'd have to listen to her then because he'd have no choice. She needed a car, and she dared not leave her mother without a vehicle again but she was willing to accept the consequences for her actions. She had always been an obedient child. Her worldview was changing though and it was time for her to take hold of the reins of her life. There was nothing her mother could do that would be any worse than not being able to see her son every morning. Nothing.

An idea formed in her mind. First, she checked the

maps app on her phone. About five hours to Dixon. Then she researched rental car companies in Abilene and found one that provided pick up service. Perfect.

She heard the blow dryer click on. Now was the time. She found her driver's license, shoved her feet back into the boots, and grabbed a jean jacket. Out the door in minutes, she ordered the pickup service and gave the rental car company her credit card. Waiting outside under the hotel awning, she couldn't hide her smile at the thought of seeing Travis and Wyatt again. Their faces were the last thing she thought about when she went to sleep and always the first thing every morning.

"We close at midnight. You called just in time," the car attendant told her as she climbed into the backseat. "Hey, you're Destynee. I heard you put on an awesome show. My wife was there with some of her friends. She's a huge fan now."

"Thank you." Standing on that stage seemed like ages ago. She wished he'd drive faster. There were no cars on the road at this time of night. Once she got the rental, if she drove hard, she could be at the front door in time to cook breakfast for her guys.

"You're all set," the sleepy-eyed associate told her as she handed Destynee the keys to a red Jeep Wrangler. "Just text or call us when you get back and we'll pick it up. You can leave the keys under the front mat."

"Does this thing drive pretty good?" She thought she could cover a lot of miles in this model.

"Turbocharged engine. It's a smooth ride, if you can stay under the radar." The lady winked.

Destynee chuckled. A ticket was the last thing she needed, but she hoped to make good time. Behind the wheel she adjusted the mirrors, set the radio dial to country music oldies, and opened the windows in an effort to stay awake. The chilly December night should help.

Setting the destination on her phone, she pulled out onto an empty highway passing under the pools of light left by the streetlights until she reached the edge of town. She breathed a sigh of relief. Nothing but the open road in front of her. The symbolism wasn't lost on her. An open road. New opportunity. A shift in her purpose. And she had five hours to make a new plan for her life. She would be in Dixon long before her mother even noticed her bed was empty.

About two hours into her road trip, Destynee switched the station from oldies to modern country. The longer she listened, pieces of her confidence chipped away. She may have a fancy website now, but what she lacked was original material. How could she make it big on country music radio singing other people's songs? The gospel songs came to the forefront of her mind. They had felt so right, touched her heart and soul. She realized her original songs could fit that market with a little tweaking. With only a few more hours to go, she pulled into an all-night gas station for a break and coffee. Maybe two coffees. As she walked to the door, she stopped in her tracks, gaping at the window. A poster. Of her.

A poster of her with that same sexy pose on the staircase advertising a show she'd be playing next week in a neighboring town. Travis must really hate her by now if he's seen any of these.

~

HER CHILDHOOD HOUSE in Dixon was dark in the pre-dawn hours as she pulled to a stop in the driveway.

Travis's pickup truck was missing. Maybe he had finally cleaned out the garage to make room for his vehicle.

Her heart felt light and happy as she hurried up the walk and banged on the front door. She could hardly wait to plant kisses on her son's face, and her husband's, too, for that matter.

No answer.

Lifting the welcome mat, the spare key was gone, of course, so she walked around to the back porch and peeked inside. The house was locked up tight and all of the lights were off. Even the side door into the garage was locked.

She finally resorted to banging on the back door, her heart skipping a beat at the thought of hearing Wyatt's cries when she woke him. "Travis! Open the door!"

Disappointment made tears sting the back of her eyes and she swallowed the lump in her throat when she didn't hear her son's cries. No one came to the door. He left. He left and took their son with him and never called her.

The realization hit and her knees buckled. She sank to the back porch steps and buried her head in her hands. Maybe it was emotions left over from the concert. Maybe it was the fact that she hadn't slept all night, or maybe the reality of her life had finally sunk in. Sobs racked her body.

Her marriage was over.

Minutes. Hours. She had no idea how long she sat hunched in the dark, hating her life. Hating Julee Rae's ridiculous ambition that she wielded over her only daughter. She dried her face using the bottom of the jean jacket and took a deep breath. Okay. What's the next move? What are you going to do now?

The only place he could possibly move to was back to

the Rafter O. She could never envision Travis getting a job and working for anybody else other than his family. It made sense. With Skip ill and on the mend, at least she hoped he was doing better, maybe they needed an extra hand. She'd go out to her in-laws' place then. She was not leaving until she talked to her husband face to face. If he was done with her, then she wanted to hear it straight from his mouth and she wanted him to say it to her face.

THE OLSENS' house at Rafter O headquarters was dark and locked up tight, too. She banged on the patio doors for several minutes, but no one answered so she sank into one of the rattan chairs. If she sat still too long, she might fall asleep, but she had to think.

It had to be Skip, her father-in-law, as to why no one was home. But why hadn't Angie called her? True, her mother had confiscated her phone for a while, but surely Julee Rae would have passed along any messages from her husband.

Wouldn't she?

As the light of a new day appeared over the Rafter O headquarters her phone buzzed. Speak of the devil.

32
DESTYNEE

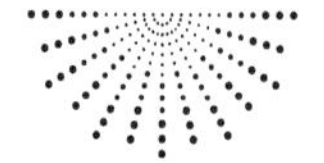

13 DAYS UNTIL CHRISTMAS

"MOTHER. CALM DOWN. I CAN EXPLAIN." Destynee held the phone away from her ear.

Except she couldn't explain because Julee Rae wouldn't let her get a word in edgewise. Her mother was furious, saying crazy things like taking away her phone again, her driver's license. Making it so she would never be alone again for the rest of her life. Even something crazy about hiring a bodyguard or some such nonsense. She was talking so fast, Destynee missed most of it.

There wasn't anything she could say to make her mother listen, so she leaned back in the chair and crossed her legs. Finally, her mother asked a question she could answer.

"I'm at the Olsens' house sitting on their patio. There's no one here either. I suppose Skip might be ill again."

She heard a sniffle and a sob.

Oh, here we go. A reminder of the sacrifices she has

made, the time and money spent in finding the right costumes, the hours spent convincing bars and churches and communities to give her baby a chance. Why would she throw it all away right when she was about to get her big break?

"I need you to come back this instant. No argument." Julee Rae's demands were precise and unyielding.

"Mother, I really need to talk to my husband."

"Get back in your car, Destynee. We have an obligation. I will not have you embarrass me like this." She could feel her mother's rage in the tone of her voice. "I expect to see you back here as soon as possible."

Destynee realized that she had crossed a line this time. Their easy going relationship would never be the same. Of course, most of that relationship centered on Destynee always doing what she was told and letting her mother have her way. It was never a question of having an adult conversation, or allowing Destynee to have any input.

But this time her mother was probably right. There was no way she would have time to drive into the city, figure out which hospital Skip might be in, and then find Travis. The only option was to head back and make it in time for a short nap, sound check, and tonight's performance.

"I'm coming back. More coffee and I'll be fine." Not that her mother even asked how she was feeling. She was a light sleeper anyway, usually functioning on only a few hours of sleep. The rest of the night she usually spent writing song lyrics on her phone while her mother slept. What a waste. It was funny really. The one night she could have had a room all to herself, and she drove away. Her mother ended the call without saying goodbye.

Rubbing her eyes, Destynee stood and then remembered an outside door under the carport that always stayed unlocked. She hurried to the side of the house. Sure enough. She was in.

First stop was the bathroom where she splashed cold water on her face and tried to come alive. All of the lights were off, with only a small light on over the sink in the kitchen. She wandered through the family room, filled with heavy leather furniture and a stone fireplace that took up one wall. At one end of the couch a basket of toys made her heart lurch. Some of them she recognized because she had bought them herself. Wandering down the hall, she peeped into Travis's old room.

They had dated since high school, so she had been invited over to the Rafter O Ranch many times. The boyhood posters were gone. Cowboy boots were lined up under the window, and in looking through the closet, she found his clothes were there. So, he had moved back in with his parents. The truth was there right in front of her.

Her body flushed with anger so intense it made her stomach lurch with nausea. She froze in the middle of the room. No phone calls. Not even a text. Hey, by the way I'm moving and taking our son with me.

When had they grown so far apart? This should have been a decision that they discussed and made together. She scanned the room again, but didn't see the baby bed, so Wyatt must have his own room.

In the bedroom directly across the hall, which used to be for one of the Olsen sisters, she couldn't remember which one, the evidence of her son made her sink to the floor on her knees. She closed her eyes and leaned her head back to take in a deep breath. It smelled like baby powder mixed with a hint of the air freshener pod next to a diaper pail.

His face floated in her mind and if she reached out her hand, she imagined he would come toddling into her arms. Her eyes snapped open when she realized the crib was gone. Instead, a low toddler bed painted to look like a tractor. On her knees, she crawled to the bed. The coolness of the pillow felt nice against her flushed cheek and the smell of toddler sweat overwhelmed her senses. The best smell in the world. Wyatt, her son.

In the opposite corner of the room a white canvas tent stood. Inside the tent cowhide-patterned pillows made a soft retreat. Stuffed animals were heaped in a pile haphazardly as though a fun free-for-all had taken place, maybe with Travis and their son at playtime. A few she remembered buying, most were not familiar. A duck, a dog and cat, an alligator. Squatting, she absentmindedly arranged them in neat rows. Tears streamed down her cheeks before she even realized it. She wiped her face and warily stood. She wanted to crawl inside that tent and hide from the world and from her mother mostly, until Travis and Wyatt could come rescue her.

Pieces of her heart were existing in a life without her. How could this be the right path for her? Too weary in spirit and in physical strength for her young years, it was all she could do to stand and walk out of that bedroom. One more show. That was it. She had a long drive to figure out what to say to her mother, and how to say it. She had to be strong and take back control of her life. No matter what she said or what she did, the outcome would not be pleasant.

Moving against the precise direction of the force that was Julee Rae would be excruciating, no doubt. Except it was the best thing for Wyatt. And that's all that mattered. Destynee had arrived to the point that she might have to sacrifice her love for music for the new love in her life. She honestly had thought that she could juggle both.

As she walked slowly towards the back door, she grabbed one of Wyatt's favorite stuffed toys, a horse they called Pinto, that lay on the coffee table in the family room. Destynee squeezed the spotted plush to her chest and closed her eyes.

"Please Lord, show me the way. Show me how to fix this broken marriage," she whispered. She wanted to add something about her music and singing for people, if it was a part of His plan, and help her become a better songwriter, a better wife, a better mother. But then God already knew all about that. He knew the secret desires of her heart, she just wished that He would hurry up and get her moving in the right direction because she had certainly made a mess of things.

She squared her shoulders, made sure the Olsens' back door closed tight behind her, and got back into the rental car. Driving away was the hardest thing Destynee had ever done in her life.

33
TRAVIS

11 DAYS UNTIL CHRISTMAS

TRAVIS HAD STAYED AT THE HOSPITAL EVERY night, and day, with his son since Sunday when they had brought him to the emergency room. He never wanted Wyatt to wake up or look around and find himself alone. If he couldn't have his mother there, Travis vowed to himself that he would always be there for Wyatt.

The young nurse that his mother knew came in the room and smiled at Wyatt.

"I see someone's awake." She went next to his bed and reached under the oxygen tent and touched his tummy. He squirmed and giggled.

Travis was in the recliner chair in a corner, his legs draped over the arm rest. Blinking his eyes, he straightened himself and cleared his throat.

"Oh, sorry, Mr. Olsen. Didn't mean to wake you."

He coughed again. "That's okay. I was half in and out all night. How's Wyatt?"

"He looks bright-eyed and awake." She touched him

again which produced more giggles. "I'm going to check his vitals and remove the oxygen tent per the doctor's orders. The doctor has released him to go home today."

"That's great," Travis said. "And thanks to you and the other staff for giving me this cot." He pointed to it folded up against the wall. "I didn't really use it. Fell asleep in the recliner instead."

As she unhooked the oxygen tent, she turned to Travis. "It's rough on parents. But thank goodness, Wyatt is doing so much better."

"Thanks to everyone who helped us. We really appreciate all your hard work."

"We're glad to do it." She smiled and continued taking down the oxygen tent.

Wyatt sat up straight in his bed. "Dada!"

"I know, buddy. I bet it's great to be out of the tent." He went to the other side of the bed and leaned in for a hug. Wyatt put his little arms around Travis's neck and squeezed.

"He's a sweetie. I'll pack up his belongings and get his clothes out so we can get him ready to go home soon. I think the doctor will be in before you go."

Travis's phone buzzed and he nudged Wyatt to settle back against the pillows. "Mom, I was just about to call you. Wyatt can come home today."

The little boy squealed and held up his hands. "Yay! Meme!"

"Yeah, that's him. All excited. No, you don't have to come. Stay there. I'll be able to bring him home. No problem. Really, Mom, just wait for us."

"Pinno! Pinno!"

The nurse shrugged and said, "He's been saying that a lot since he's been here. I'm not sure what he means."

"Hold on, Mom. Wyatt's saying something." To his boy, "What is it, Wyatt?"

"Pinno! Pinno! Horsie."

"What? Oh, Pinto. Is that what you want?"

Then to his mother still holding on the other end, "I think he's asking for one of his stuffed animals. Mom, will you look for the Pinto horse? I'll tell him it's waiting for him at home."

He held on while his mother walked from one room to the next.

"Mom, you don't have to go in there now—"

But of course she did. Travis put her on speaker just so he could hear her better.

"Almost there. Okay. Well, that's weird," she said.

"What is?"

"All his stuffed animals."

"What's wrong with them?"

"They're all organized. Real neat. In rows."

"So?"

"I haven't been here since we took Wyatt to the hospital. I didn't do this. It was a mess last time I saw it."

"Maybe Angie straightened up."

"Oh, sure. Your sister has had her hands full at the barn. It's just really weird. Gave me a chill like someone's been in here."

"Who else would go in there? Well, don't worry about it. I've got to go. We'll be home soon." And then in a whisper so Wyatt couldn't hear. "And find that Pinto horse, Mom."

"I'll do my best. Be careful driving home, Son."

"Will do."

As Travis helped Wyatt get into his shirt and pants,

Doctor Mercedez entered the room. "Well, my little friend, are you ready to go home?"

"Yay!" Wyatt gave her a big smile.

"He's doing so much better," the doctor said to Travis. "I must say, it's kind of a miracle. Some kids take longer to recuperate. But his lungs sound clear, no temp, and no cough. You must have a strong group of praying people around you."

"It's my mother. She has a direct line to God, I think."

They both laughed.

"Well," the doc said, "it's good to have that kind of person in your corner. Do you know what G.O.K. means?"

Travis wrinkled his brow and repeated, "Gok?"

"G.O.K. When physicians are faced with an unexplainable cure or outcome they sometimes enter that on a patient's chart. God Only Knows."

Travis was silent and just stared into her eyes. "Wow. That's pretty cool."

He thanked the doctor and nurse and finished dressing Wyatt.

But filed that little God story away in his head. He didn't wear his faith out in public the way his mother did, but he did believe in God. And if prayer or a miracle had something to do with his son getting better so quickly, he was certainly grateful.

"Come on, Wyatt, you ready to go home?"

"Yes, Dada!"

The nurse came around with a wheelchair to escort them out.

"What's that for?" Travis asked.

"It's policy."

"You don't want me in it, do you? I'm not sick."

She smiled. "No, but with our little patients, sometimes the parent sits in the chair with the child on his or her lap."

"Uh, that's not gonna happen." He looked at his son. "Wyatt, do you want to go for a ride?"

"Yeah, Dada!"

Travis placed him in the chair and the nurse added a folded up blanket next to him so he wouldn't slide around.

"Now sit real still and hold on. I'm right here and we're going to wheel you out. Stay in the chair until I tell you to get out. Okay?"

"Kay, Dada!"

Riding down the hallway, Wyatt waved to every person he saw, gave a big smile, and said, "Home!" Staff and others clapped. A couple people even gave his little hand a high five.

Outside Travis's truck was waiting at the curb after he had brought it around a few minutes earlier.

He thanked the nurse again. "His personality is still intact. He's never met a stranger."

She moved the wheelchair to the side and said to Wyatt as his dad fitted him into the car seat. "Goodbye, little man. I'm glad you're feeling better. Take care of yourself. And your dad."

"Mama!" Wyatt said. He never forgot his mother.

"All the best," she said to Travis and wheeled the chair back inside.

Travis hit the button for music in his truck and headed toward home.

He looked back at Wyatt. "You doin' okay, buddy?"

"Yeah, Dada."

Travis watched him in the rearview mirror. Sometimes Wyatt mouthed the words and tried to sing along.

Other times he gazed out the window, almost pensive as though he had something on his little mind.

"Moo!" He pointed out the window at some cows and giggled.

They had gotten pretty close to the ranch and luckily there were few cars, when suddenly Travis braked for something sitting in the middle of the road.

"What is that? Not trash."

He pulled the truck to the side of the road.

"I'll be darned," he said. "You sit right there, Wyatt. Dada has to look at something. I'll be right back."

He had grabbed a blanket from the backseat and walked to the center of the street.

"What are you doing out here alone?" He looked around and asked again. "Where's your mother? You got any brothers or sisters around?"

Whimpering, with big brown eyes, a spotted puppy dog looked up at him, shivering the whole time.

"Cold, aren't ya? Well, don't bite me with those little sharp teeth and I'll wrap you in this blanket."

Just like with horses, Travis had a soft heart for all animals. He couldn't leave it out here by itself. It wouldn't survive. He'd bring it home, doctor it if need be, and find it a home.

The puppy wiggled, wagged its tail, and cried some more. Travis wrapped it up and searched both sides of the road for signs of any more dogs but found nothing. Maybe some jerk had dumped this one.

He headed back to his truck and decided he'd set the dog on the passenger seat. It was so small and wrapped good, it probably wouldn't move around much. Hopefully, Wyatt wouldn't make a fuss over it.

But that wasn't going to happen. Wyatt must've

caught a glimpse of the puppy's body. Spotted brown and white.

"Dada!" He exclaimed as his dad drove down the road. "Pinno! Pinno!"

Travis laughed. "No, buddy, this isn't your Pinto horse. He's back home. This is a lost puppy. We're gonna take him home."

"Pinno! Me hold Pinno!"

"No, buddy, not right now. Dada has to drive. We'll be home soon. Then you can look at him."

Quietly, with a pouty lip, Wyatt said, "Pinno."

AT HOME, Travis got his son out of the car seat and held him in one arm. With the other he scooped up the blanketed pup. He tapped the front door with his boot and also tried turning the doorknob.

Grace opened the door and exclaimed, "Great! You're home. Wyatt! Here, I can take him, Travis. What else are you carrying?"

They came through the door and Wyatt took to squealing and jabbering. He wriggled out of Grace's arms and ran to Pappy who was in the recliner.

"What in the world is going on, buddy?" Skip asked.

"Pinno! Pinno! Pinno!"

Grace looked to Travis and shrugged. She mouthed, "I can't find it."

"Mom, I don't think he's talking about his horse. It's this." And he uncovered the puppy in his arms.

"What is that?" She was shocked, but a huge smile took over her face. "Wyatt, who is this?"

"Pinno!"

Travis tried to explain. "It was in the middle of the

road, abandoned. I couldn't just leave it there. I figure we can clean him up, see if he's hurt, and find him a home."

"My Pinno!"

Grace tried to conceal her smile and just shrugged again. Travis rolled his eyes.

"Wyatt, are you hungry? Why don't I get you some chicken nuggets and juice?"

"Kay, Meme."

Then he hugged his Pappy again and told him all about the lady at the hospital. "Da Mercy." No matter how many times Travis or Grace told him her name was Doctor Mercedez, Wyatt wanted to just say Mercy. So, they let him. Grace smiled. "We were certainly given mercy, a real gift with a good prognosis. And now it looks like Santa may have brought another surprise gift. This spotty one with the wagging tail."

34
DESTYNEE

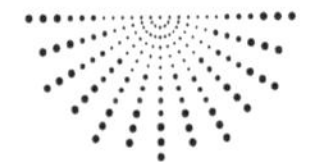

10 DAYS UNTIL CHRISTMAS

TYPICAL TEXAS BAR SCENE. MIDNIGHT RODEO featured a sea of cowboy hats worn by men who'd never seen the sunrise from a saddle. They were there for the girls. Long hair, fake eyelashes, fringed mini-skirts, western boots with the sole purpose of two-stepping, and more than a few fake ID cards. It was a college town so the crowd was lively and ready to party. Nobody was there for Destynee or her music.

Seeing them made her miss her own cowboy even more. Travis used to play his guitar at the dances after the local rodeos and was always with her. Now that she thought about it, there was never any discussion of him even coming along with her on this holiday tour. After Destynee had the baby, her mother said it was time to hit the road, and she never questioned the timing or considered any other options.

She trudged through the laughter and chatter towards the back to find a dressing room where she could be alone. Sometimes it was an actual space for the talent with a couch and snacks. Oftentimes it was merely one corner in a storage closet.

Taped to the white cinder block wall a hand-lettered sign read "Stage" and "Dressing Rooms" with arrows pointing the way. She turned right. Behind a red door with chipped paint and gouges in the wood, she dropped her carryall on the floor and sunk into the cheap vinyl chair.

Destynee was beginning to unravel. All her life she had felt blessed to have a detail-oriented mother who cared about her career. Julee Rae had managed her performance calendar and she dutifully had shown up, performed, and smiled without question. She loved every part of it. Now she had doubts. Was this the path God wanted for her? If she was living her best life, why would she have so many misgivings and guilt? Her husband was raising their child alone. That was not how she had ever imagined her life would be. It just didn't make sense. And even after that long car drive with plenty of time to think, she still had questions and doubts.

She didn't even bother to apply makeup or brush her hair. Ignoring the mirror, she lifted her guitar out of the case and tuned on it a bit. The singing would come easy. She'd start with a Patsy Cline song to warm up the crowd, and then sing the popular covers that everyone could dance to. But tonight, she was going to end with something different. An old-time gospel tune perhaps or a more modern praise and worship song. She felt a lightness in her chest in anticipation. Just because she felt as though her life was going down a dark hole didn't mean she had to leave her audience with the same feeling. She'd end on a high note. Chasing the light.

Her mother had stayed at the motel and she had

driven herself to the bar. Julee Rae had phone calls to make and a conference call scheduled with Lucius and his team. "All this hard work is for you, Destynee. You should appreciate us all more than you do."

Another reason to feel guilty. She had no idea how much Lucius and his team were costing because Julee Rae took care of the bookings and the money. Destynee wondered if her name was even on the account. She was relieved though, because now she could sing whatever she wanted in whatever order. The longer she thought about it, the more the stress melted away. She should relax and enjoy the spotlight for once.

A tap at her door, and then it opened to reveal a pink-haired girl in black-rimmed glasses. "You're on after the opening band, in about thirty or forty-five minutes, give or take. Then you'll close the show. Can you handle that?"

Destynee blinked. What a strange inquiry. Aggressive and down to business. "Yes, ma'am, I can." She couldn't think of any other way to answer that question.

"Sometimes we've had singers that were all hype and no substance, if you know what I mean. You have a great website and all, and you're very pretty but the boss took a real chance on you. I hope you can deliver because you ain't cheap." Before Destynee could reply the door shut in her face. That last comment certainly piqued her curiosity.

Now that was news to her. How much was she getting paid per gig? And was that a challenge? She dug into her carry all and found the makeup bag, carefully applying everything she brought and then some. She dug out her brush, curling iron, styling gel, and finished off her hairdo with extra hairspray. That should do it. Normally she didn't bother with jewelry, but this time she went all out. Dangling earrings, stacked sparkling bracelets. and while she got ready, she rethought her lineup of songs. She'd give them a show they'd not soon forget.

And that's exactly what she did. The audience gave back—not one, but two encores. So she took that as a direct message from God to use the opportunity to sing two gospel songs. Even though it was late and most everybody was probably three sheets to the wind, they loved it. Many sang along, their voices filling the space and overpowering her guitar. She had never had more fun.

Destynee left the stage under exuberant applause and whistles, bouncing into her dressing room to catch her breath, joyfulness in her heart. She found a box of tissues to wipe the sweat from her face. She had given it her all. Her throat was a bit scratchy, and she could feel the strain on her vocal cords. She had already forgotten the schedule, but maybe there would be enough time to rest if she didn't talk the rest of the night and all day tomorrow.

The knock on her door startled her, and, before she could answer, it swung open wide. The hall was bulged with smiling faces and hands thrusted towards her.

"Can I have your autograph?"

"I'm your biggest fan."

Laughing, she walked into the throng. She just smiled and signed her name and smiled some more. It wasn't even a strain on her voice. They never noticed that she didn't utter a word.

As the last of the fans dwindled, she noticed the band members who had played before her hanging around the stage talking to a few of the waitresses and the girl with the pink hair. Smiling at them, too, she went back into her dressing room. Another knock on the door brought a smile to her face, so she grabbed an ink pen and opened the door ready to sign her name again. Her hand was cramped but she didn't mind.

A familiar looking young man dressed in black stood at the threshold, matched her smile, and walked inside her dressing room right past her. She stiffened.

"We met before," he said, offering a hand, but then got close and hugged her. "I'm Gunther. It was at the holiday jamboree several weeks, or maybe days ago. I can't remember." He laughed. She caught a whiff of his tobacco breath tinged by alcohol.

She didn't answer, but stiffened and did not return the hug.

"I just wanted to tell you how much I enjoyed your singing."

"Thank you, but if you don't mind, I'm really tired. Maybe I'll catch you again on the road sometime." He did not step away. He got so close that she had to push firmly on his chest to edge him towards the door, but it was like pushing against a brick wall.

"Awww, don't be like that."

"Excuse me?" Her voice sounded breathless and her legs trembled, but she kept the smile on her face.

"That mini skirt looked fine in your promo pictures. I'm thinking you might be needing some attention. And I know how lonely it gets out here on the road. Can't you be nice to me?" He dropped his voice to a whisper. "Destynee. Come on now."

"I am a wife and mother, and you need to leave right now."

"I don't care about that. Nobody has to know." He grabbed both shoulders and pulled her in for a kiss. She turned her head just in time, and his lips landed on her neck. He smiled and pushed her back against the counter, closing in on the other side of her neck. His lips seared her skin and made her stomach convulse. That's when she screamed. The sound came out pitiful and shallow because of her sore throat.

Reaching behind, her hand gripped the only thing within reach. A curling iron. Lifting it slowly, she suddenly gave it her all and the metal landed just above his ear with a thwack. He hollered and she ran to open the door wide. This time her scream was solid and loud. Several people hanging backstage turned their heads, and the girl with the pink hair came running. Destynee pointed into her dressing room where Gunther was still doubled over holding the side of his head.

"What's going on in here?" she asked.

"Nothing. I was just leaving." Gunther made a dash down the hall and disappeared before Destynee could even catch her breath. She was paralyzed, trying to slow her beating heart. All she could think about was Travis. She needed her husband's arms around her. She needed his warmth and protection.

"Do you want to press charges?"

"What?"

The girl with the pink hair stared at her. "Are you okay? I said, do you want to press charges? I can call the police and you can fill out an assault report."

"No. I'm fine." But she wasn't fine and she didn't know what to do about it.

"If you're ready to leave, I'll have someone walk you to your car."

"Yes, please. I'd appreciate it."

"And Destynee. Thanks for being here. You put on one heck of a show."

She smiled but couldn't talk because of the lump in

her throat and the ringing in her ears. It was all that she could do to not burst into tears. One of the young men who had operated the lightboard carried her guitar case and walked her to the car. She started the engine, but didn't put it in drive, instead, shivered as the heater struggled to warm up. The parking light lots suddenly blurred and she realized her eyes were full of tears. Turning on the dome light, she searched through the carryall for a tissue as tears streamed down her face, and then she looked in the console, too. There wasn't a tissue anywhere to be found which made her cry harder.

Travis wasn't there to comfort her, so she sat there and cried instead.

35
DESTYNEE

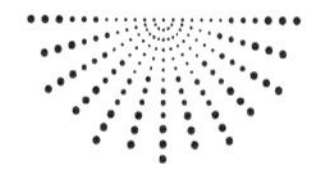

THE PARKING LOT OF THE MIDNIGHT RODEO emptied out and Destynee remained in her car. Staring at the pools of light that formed on the blacktop and watching the taillights of the last car until they disappeared into the dark night. It had to be after one o'clock in the morning, and she really needed a cup of hot tea and sleep. But she could not bring herself to put the car in drive. She did not want to see her mother, or explain why her hands were still shaking.

Where was her phone? She wanted to talk to Travis. And she wanted to talk to her mother. She had to make a change or she was going to have a nervous breakdown. Tonight had made that very clear to her. For the first time in her life, her priorities were no longer the same. She had to find the courage to make a change. She had a young son who needed her. She needed him, too. And a husband who she had exchanged vows with. Their life together had only just begun before it was torn apart.

"Stop being such a whimpering coward," she told herself.

With a heavy sigh, she buckled her seatbelt and slowly accelerated out of the parking lot. The motel wasn't far. She could see the illuminated sign rising above the buildings. Weary to the bone, she parked, grabbed her bag and guitar case. It was all she could do to drag herself through the lobby towards the elevators. She noticed the complimentary coffee and hot water was still sitting out, so she stopped to make herself a cup of lemon and ginger herb tea. With the bag looped over one shoulder, she carefully held the hot paper cup while carrying her guitar case with the other hand.

"Let me get that for you," the night desk clerk offered to push the elevator button.

"Four, please," she murmured.

Instead of digging through her pockets and billfold in search of the room key, she knocked.

The door swung open. "Oh good. I waited up for you. We need to talk." Julee Rae stepped aside to allow Destynee to come in and then took the guitar case from her hand.

"Yes, Mother, we do need to talk." She collapsed on the bed, changing hands with her hot tea before taking another sip.

"I have exciting news that I've been waiting to share."

"Okay." Looks like her mother was going first.

"I have tried and tried and finally succeeded. All of our dreams are coming true."

Whatever could she mean?

"I have been calling and calling and calling, and finally. I got through! You, my lovely daughter, have a spot next Monday at The Stardust Café. In Nashville!"

"What?" A cold chill etched its way up Destynee's spine.

"First twenty-five callers and I finally got us in. You're

on. You have a performance tomorrow night in Fort Worth, Friday, and then we'll have two days to get there for your open mic debut. It's going to be a long drive, but with both of us taking turns we can do it." Julee Rae actually clapped her hands and spun around in one place. "I'm so excited. This is everything we've always wanted."

Destynee blinked. She couldn't think of anything to say.

"Aren't you going to thank me?" Her mother stopped the giddiness to stand with hands on her hips. "Aren't you going to say anything at all?"

"My throat," Destynee croaked.

"Oh no! Don't talk. You need to save your voice. This is awful."

Destynee stared at her mother, not daring to utter a word. This news certainly took the wind out of her sails. How could she not do this one final thing for her mother?

Instead of trying to talk, she sipped the hot tea Julee Rae had fixed and let the warm liquid soothe her irritated throat. The Stardust Café. In Nashville. She never ever dreamed of such an opportunity. It was an iconic place. Historical. Where a lot of new singers got their start.

"It's all set. I've received confirmation, and you don't need to worry about a thing. I'll handle everything. You just focus on healing your throat. We need to talk about what you'll wear. And Lucius is flying in tomorrow to do a quick promo shoot. We're going to take advantage of this and get the word out everywhere."

Julee Rae dug around in a woven shoulder bag to produce a pack of menthol cough drops. She opened the package and dropped one in Destynee's tea.

"I used to do this when my singing voice was

strained. It works. Here's a bottle of water. Drink it before bedtime, and then gargle with hot saltwater. I'll set the salt shaker in the bathroom."

Destynee opened her mouth to respond but from the look on Julee Rae's face, she nodded her head instead.

"Tomorrow we will discuss what you'll wear and the songs you'll sing. I want to include Lucius on this as well. I'm sure he'll have some good suggestions."

That's great but what about her ideas?

The very first person she needed to talk to, when she dared speak any words again, was Travis. Too exhausted to look for her phone, she slipped her boots off, propped herself up on pillows, and finished her tea. Still shaken from the attack, she focused on breathing although her insides still trembled. The idea came to her that she should change into her pajamas, but never moved another muscle. It was her husband's face that floated in her mind as she drifted off to sleep.

36
DESTYNEE

9 DAYS UNTIL CHRISTMAS

DESTYNEE WOKE TO CLATTERING OF SOMETHING hitting the floor. Gasping for air she tried to still her pounding heart. She sat straight up in bed. Her insides trembled from the sudden remembered sensation of hot breath on her neck and a body pressed against hers. Fear made her dizzy for a moment. She blinked. It was a hotel room.

"Oh, sorry," her mother said. "I didn't mean to wake you. Why are you so jumpy?"

She shoved the covers back and then realized she still wore the same clothes and was in the same position as the night before.

"How did the performance go last night? I'm sorry I wasn't there, but I did get caught on phone calls and answering emails. Lucius has some great ideas for your Nashville costume. He's working on it right away." Her mother squealed. "Oooooh, I can't believe I just said that. You're going to Nashville, sweetheart. All of our dreams are coming true!"

Destynee swallowed. Her throat felt better. "That's what I want to talk to you about, Mother."

"Talk about what?" Her mother stashed clothes into a suitcase, and then moved into the bathroom where the counter was covered with cosmetics. She placed those in her carryall, a bag as big as the one for her clothing.

"Mother." Destynee swallowed and took a breath. Courage. You can do this. "I'm thinking Nashville might be my last performance for a while. What would you think about taking a break?"

"Nonsense. I've got us scheduled dates right up through the holidays and into the New Year. After Monday night, more doors will open than you can ever imagine. Just you wait and see."

"That's just it, Mother. I'm not sure I can keep going. I'm not sure I want to."

Julee Rae spun around with a shocked look on her face. "Of course, you can. It's that little throat thing that has you scared. I'll fix you another cup of tea. You relax, while I finish packing."

She filled a plastic cup from the faucet, dropped a tea bag in the liquid, and placed it in the microwave. At the beep, she opened the door and dropped another throat lozenge in the cup.

Defeated before she had even begun, Destynee accepted the tea and leaned back against the headboard. She watched in silence as her mother bustled around and began taking their luggage to the car. The tea did nothing to fill the empty feeling in the pit of her stomach or to erase the overwhelming dread that now hung over her head like a gloomy shadow. What was wrong with her? She loved singing.

"Let's go. We need to get on the road to Fort Worth."

Inwardly, Destynee groaned but she didn't argue. Always the dutiful daughter, she skirted around her mother for a shower. One thing for certain, she was glad to leave Abilene behind.

TRUE TO HIS WORD, Lucius was on the red eye flight and met them in Fort Worth at the stockyards. He commanded attention when he walked into the room, an assistant and photographer following close behind. She had to admit that he did have some brilliant ideas which he relayed with genuine enthusiasm. The man knew his business. He was also a name dropper about the stars who owed him their success. Destynee couldn't read him though. She wasn't sure if what he said was true or not. She didn't dislike the man, she just didn't have the same type of vision for her career that he and Julee Rae seemed to share.

They had planned a whirlwind afternoon. Her mother produced several costumes, which made Destynee wonder when she had had time to go shopping. Lucius wanted to do at least two different locations. First, the stockyards with boots and jeans, but when he told her to tie her T-shirt up higher so that her stomach would show, she refused.

"You really should get a belly button ring," he said. "That would give you an edgy vibe."

She looked at him, her face reflecting nothing.

"A tattoo would be even better," he said.

She didn't want to be edgy or sexy or hip. She didn't want to be any of those things. She just wanted to be Destynee, a wife and a mother who loved to sing. But she did what he told her to do without uttering a word, mainly because it was two against one and she'd never win, and secondly, for fear that her voice would give out any minute.

Julee Rae had booked her at the Thirsty Longhorn that night, and then early in the morning they would hit the road for Nashville.

"A ten-hour drive and interstate all the way, and no talking," her mother had said.

The second location for the photo shoot was inside one of the bars located at the stockyards. A suede skirt, boots, and a silky top didn't make her feel uncomfortable. But when Lucius had her sit on the bar, legs crossed, with a half-smile on her face, she inwardly didn't like the attention. Why did this have to be part of her career? Couldn't they just let her sing?

"Just keep that outfit on and I'll drive you to the venue from here," Julee Rae said.

Then, turning to face Lucius she smiled widely "That was spectacular. You do such good work."

"Thank you, love. Always a pleasure working with you."

They embraced and then Lucius walked over to Destynee. "You are a strikingly beautiful girl with the voice of an angel. It's your attitude that needs some work, but I do enjoy collaborating with you."

She did offer him a half smile and said goodbye. Collaboration? Not really. No one had asked her opinion on anything. She watched him walk away, and almost called out to his back. What she really wanted to say was that he had certainly hit the nail on the head. It was absolutely her attitude, and she felt bad that others could notice.

37
TRAVIS

8 DAYS UNTIL CHRISTMAS

TRAVIS STOOD FROZEN IN PLACE, STARING AT the ten-foot Christmas tree in his parents' family room. Conflicting emotions kept him there, mesmerized by the ornaments he had made in Sunday school as a kid. Remembering past Christmases with his brothers and sisters. And now facing what should be one of the most joyous Christmases ever with his incredible toddler, he had never felt more alone. The other half of his soul was missing.

He imagined Destynee feeling just as lonely as he did, sitting backstage thinking about him and Wyatt. Dreading the monotony that had become of her life living out of hotel rooms, moving from town to town.

"It turned out nice, didn't it?" Grace stopped beside him and placed an arm around his waist.

Travis cleared his throat in an effort to tap down the emotions that threatened to rise to the surface. It did nothing. He had to wait another minute until he could find his voice.

"It looks great, Mom. You and Angie did a good job."

"I wish Destynee could be here. Have you heard from her?"

"No, I haven't." His jaw clenched.

"Have you tried to contact her?"

Travis snapped his head around and looked at her.

"I know how you can be. I've lived with you most of your life. You can be a stubborn man, Travis." Disapproval showed on her face. "You don't like confrontation and you hide your emotions."

He broke eye contact and turned to look at the tree again. "My wife is a grown woman. She needs to decide on what kind of life she wants. I can't make that decision for her."

"I'm not sure she has a choice in all of this. Have you ever asked her?" Grace patted his back. "Love you, Son. I know that you'll do what's best for your family."

Her comment shocked him. Now that he thought about it, he and Destynee never once discussed this ridiculous holiday touring schedule. Julee Rae said, "Let's go" And Destynee got in the car. Julee Rae gave him instructions on what needed to be done in the house. He and Wyatt stood on the front porch and waved goodbye. He wracked his brain. Had there ever been a real discussion about what Destynee wanted? What would be good for their family?

The answer was a resounding no. Maybe his mother was right. Destynee was the most non-confrontational person he knew, just like him. They rarely argued. Always the peacemaker, always the first to say, "I'm sorry," even if she had no reason to apologize. She went out of her way to make sure everyone was stress-free and had what they needed, particularly when it came to keeping her mother happy.

And her devotion to Wyatt was unlike anything he'd ever seen. That's why it surprised him when she got in the car for that string of dates her mother had already booked. And it surprised him when she left the hospital after visiting his dad without a backwards glance. She had to have been upset after seeing Wyatt.

His son suddenly toddled into the room with grandpa close behind hanging on to one hand. "We made it down the hall and into each bedroom. He is exploring every nook and cranny now that he's mobile." Skip laughed.

"That good exercise for both of you," Grace called out from the kitchen.

"Whoa now," Travis said as he blocked his son's chubby hand from trying to reach a glittery angel. Grace had left ornaments off the lowest branches, but that didn't mean his son had lost interest in trying. "No, Wyatt."

Skip handed him a stuffed buffalo. "Here, Wyatt. You can play with this."

Wyatt took the toy and then threw it at his grandpa. Travis was about to discipline him, but Skip laughed. "He has an arm on him. Future pitcher for the Dixon Bulldogs, I'm thinking."

"Mama," said Wyatt, as he cast a glance towards the front door. The adults froze. A sadness broke the happy mood. There was nothing he could do to fix the need his son had to see his mother again.

Travis shook his head. "I'm going to finish my rounds and put out salt blocks."

"Here's a thermos of coffee to take with you, and a few chocolate chip cookies that just came out of the oven." His mother met him at the back door as he shoved his arms into a canvas jacket. He gave her a weak smile and then shoved a hat on his head.

Wyatt grunted and held out a chubby hand as he looked at his grandmother with wide, pleading eyes.

"That boy is so observant when there's a cookie anywhere around." Grace broke off a piece and handed him a bite.

38
DESTYNEE

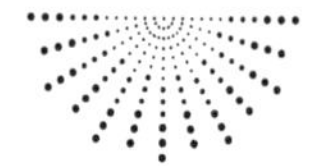

8 DAYS UNTIL CHRISTMAS

DESTYNEE HAD NEVER SEEN HER MOTHER MORE excited about anything. Their Pontiac was eating up miles on the way from Texas to Nashville for her spot in the Monday night open mic event at the Stardust Café. They had two days to get there.

Country music oldies played softly on the radio, not so loud that it drowned out any conversation but enough to break the monotony of the drive. For the first time in her life, Julee Rae talked about her early days trying to break into the business, spurred perhaps by her good mood, which was rare, and by the artists and songs on the radio. She had a story to tell about almost every singer, a chance encounter, a dinner or studio party. And maybe because Destynee was married and a mother now, Julee Rae talked about the people she dated, the longest being a famous record producer. The timeline was confusing. She had rambled so much.

Destynee remembered her father with full clarity.

Handsome. Sandy colored hair. He tickled her and made her laugh. He seemed kind. Julee Rae was gone a lot trying to get her singing career off the ground, so he spent time taking care of Destynee. But one day he was there, and then one day he wasn't. After that it was just her and her mother. Destynee wondered what the real story was but her mother wouldn't talk about it, only called him a jerk and said he wanted her to be a housewife and left them. Was that the truth?

"We'll be at The Ryman within the next year, mark my words." Julee Rae talked with her hands when she was excited. "Lucius will get us there. I just know it. I have faith in that young man."

Destynee wondered if she should take over the driving what with all her mother's gestures. That last comment about Lucius being responsible for her success made her want to argue, but she held her tongue. Could it possibly have anything to do with her singing ability? She clenched her jaw in frustration.

"Now, what are you going to sing?" Julee Rae turned off the radio. "Let's go over a few ideas that I have. Don't talk too much. Conserve your voice."

Over the next several hours, her mother called out a song, and Destynee would sing it. But low, not all out like she would on stage. She had always had a photographic memory. One time through a song and she remembered every word. It wasn't until she was much older that she learned not everyone had that ability.

"There will only be twenty-five artists and you must make your time in the spotlight count. You cannot mess this up, Destynee. Song selection is everything."

She hummed a few bars and then went into another Patsy Cline staple. Her voice seemed to suit the music of that era better than anything else. This time, for the first time, her mother sang along. At the first hint of harmony, she turned her head sharply in surprise but kept singing.

"You have a beautiful voice, Mother!"

"Why would that surprise you? I had a record deal by the time I was eighteen." Julee Rae shrugged her shoulders.

"But you've never sung with me before. You could have been singing harmony this whole time. We could have been on the stage together."

"No. I'm past my prime, and besides I enjoy the business side of the entertainment industry. I've learned so much over the years. We'll get more places with you singing, not me."

Julee Rae stopped at a fast-food chain where they took a restroom break and placed an order to go. Destynee offered to drive, but her mother insisted they would get there faster if she did. "You drive under the speed limit most of the time. It causes me stress."

After they had finished eating, her mother held out her phone. "Dial Lucius for me."

Destynee placed the call and put him on speaker, and then the song list was discussed again at length. If he wasn't familiar with a song, which counted for most of them, Destynee had to sing the first few lines, still gently and not full on. It annoyed her that the publicist her mother had hired knew little to nothing about country music. They had just seen him in Fort Worth. They couldn't possible have that much to talk about.

Once again, they talked like she wasn't even there, never once asking her thoughts on anything. Except for Lucius who had an opinion on everything, to which her mother listened intently and agreed. Suddenly the realization of what he was proposing dawned on Destynee.

He was a publicist of a different caliber than she had ever experienced before. How much were they paying him anyway?

Next topic was a lengthy telephone discussion on what she should wear and what kind of image they wanted to portray. After Lucius finally hung up, Destynee got her chance to change to subject.

"I need some money for Christmas shopping." She watched her mother's reaction closely. A quick frown and then it was back to her emotionless face. Julee Rae would make an outstanding poker player.

"That's sweet, dear, but I don't need anything."

"For my son, Mother. And my husband." Irritation made her belly ache. She needed an antacid. "And I'm thinking about mailing a few notes and a token of thanks to a few of the people who have been such great hosts these last few months. We couldn't have done this without them."

"We are on a very tight budget, Destynee. You need to rein the spending in as much as you can."

First of all, there was nothing to rein in because Destynee never had time to shop. Secondly, the new leather purse her mother now carried came to mind, at least a three-hundred-dollar purchase. A comment was on the tip of her tongue, but she stayed quiet. Guilt pricked her mind, too. She had amassed some beautiful performance outfits during this tour, and most obviously not from secondhand stores which they had relied on in the early days of her career. But having a child had changed her focus.

"You know, Travis barely makes enough to cover expenses for diapers, food, and gasoline. I want to give Wyatt a good Christmas this year."

"Pffftt. Your husband doesn't have any expenses. I'm

letting him live in my house for free and that baby of yours barely eats anything. If Travis gets hungry, he can always go eat with his parents. They'll feed him."

Destynee felt her face flush with anger. Actually, Travis had been told to live in her mother's house and she hadn't taken his side on anything when it came to her mother, which was probably why he moved out and took her son with him. But that was a topic for another day. Back to the dollars and cents, which was foremost on her mind.

"How much money do I have in my account, Mother?"

"I'm not really sure."

"How can you not know? You're my business manager and you handle all the funds. I never see a check or a contract. How much did I make on that last performance where they bumped me from one song to four? Did I get a bonus for that?" Destynee recalled a bonus being mentioned, but her mother was denying it now.

"That was several days ago, sweetheart. I don't remember."

"How much are we paying Lucius?"

That caused a rise out of her. With lips pursed tight and eyes narrowed, she didn't answer for several minutes. "He gets a percentage and I'm not certain on how it's calculated. But he is worth his weight in gold, I tell you."

"I need some answers. I need to know if this is worth my time, or are we spending everything that I generate?"

A pout formed on her mother's face. "I just don't understand why you're questioning me about this. It's not like you, Destynee. You know that everything I do is for you and you alone. It is my dream to see you reach your potential in this industry."

She even managed to brush her cheek with the back of her hand. Fake tears. Her mother should have pursued an acting career. Here we go. She can sure lay on the guilt. Destynee wasn't even sure whose dream it was anymore.

Julee Rae turned on her blinker and took the next exit. "Let's get an ice cream. I'm still famished. And you should really conserve your voice."

"I'm fine. Can I see the bank statements?" She focused on staying calm, but she felt her blood pressure building.

"I can't talk about this right now. I've got to concentrate on the traffic. It's a mess. You don't want us to get in a wreck, do you?"

Destynee remained silent through their treat and for several miles thereafter. Fuming. Thinking about how to word the questions and get the answers she wanted. Maybe she should call the bank and ask for a balance. Was her name even on the account? And then she realized she did not know the bank they used. She remembered signing paperwork for a new account, but the name escaped her.

Julee Rae turned the radio back on, obviously avoiding her daughter's prying questions. Instead of bringing up the subject again, Destynee got out her phone and put in her earbuds.

One post from Angie popped up into her feed. She smiled at the photos. The annual holiday open house at the Wild Cow Ranch, a Creek County tradition for many years until the owners had both passed. The lights in the trees caught her eye first. Obviously, their granddaughter Carli was making an effort for bigger and better. That made her happy, and she hated to have missed it this year. She was about to remind her mother of the times they had gone when a picture caught her eye. Wyatt's smile. Her little boy.

The biggest grin she had ever seen on her son's face as he sat on the back of a donkey. Wyatt again petting a llama, of all things. Even a short video of Wyatt squealing as he leaned forward, lips puckered in an attempt to kiss a kitten. Laughter from a group of people, but she couldn't see who they were. Another picture with that horrible babysitter holding him on the back of a miniature pony. Destynee caught herself. Maybe she was just jealous and homesick. She didn't really know the girl.

Her favorite was of her toddler son standing in the shadows looking up at a tree filled with white lights, his face illuminated, a knit cap covering his head with eyes transfixed and wide with wonder, tiny legs with boots, cutest things ever, poking out from a puffy coat. No doubt Grace had bought those boots for him. Even though her heart ached, she had to smile.

She kept scrolling down, and then decided to go directly to Angie's page to see if she had posted more picture of Wyatt that hadn't shown up in her own feed. There was another video of Wyatt standing in front of the living Nativity that the Wild Cow had every year.

And then she gasped. Wyatt under an oxygen tent. In the hospital? In her post, Angie asked for prayers for her little nephew. Shock and disbelief made Destynee pause. She couldn't take her eyes off the picture of her son. She could see tear tracks on his face, his eyes wide with fright. An arm was in the photo. A hand resting on the shoulder of her toddler son. It was Travis. She recognized the shirt fabric. At least Wyatt has his father by his side.

No one had called her? No. One.

The air left her chest and she couldn't suppress the sob that escaped her lips. Thank goodness the music was loud. Her mother didn't even notice. Destynee thought she might choke. It was all she could do not to scream from the intensity of emotion that assaulted her. What did it matter? They didn't want her to be a part of the family. She realized that now that Travis had moved on and never told her. Not one missed call. Not one text message. Even when her son was sick enough to be in the hospital, her own husband had not called her.

She had chosen this path but she was about to unchoose it. She had one more performance obligation and then she was done. The absolute feeling of rejection and betrayal was overwhelming. She was broken, and at this point she didn't know if she could ever recover.

39
TRAVIS

7 DAYS UNTIL CHRISTMAS

TRAVIS SAT ON STRAWBERRY, HIS FAVORITE RED roan mare, from an overlook and surveyed the Rafter O winter pasture. The ranch, Olsen land for as far he could see, stretched to the horizon in every direction under a perfect blue sky with the sun directly overhead like a centerpiece. Thankful to God that he and his family were fortunate to be caretakers of this land. He came by it naturally, this love of the treeless land and endless sky. It was in his genes.

A cold front had moved through the night before blanketing the brown grass with a dusting of white. He could feel the stress slipping away. This ranch would always be his place of peace and riding would always be his favorite pastime.

Travis's parents used to tell him stories about how Grace rode when she was pregnant with him. Actually, she did with all their kids, but more so when Travis, her youngest, came along. She didn't ride now so much, although she could, but she was older and busy with grown children, a couple of grands, and the community.

They always said that's where Travis got his love of horses, from his mom. He couldn't get enough of them. When he was no bigger than Wyatt, he'd sit in front of Grace on the saddle, squealing, laughing, and having the time of his life. She'd make the horse walk slow and hold onto him tight.

Anyone could see what a natural he was, no fear. And all through his growing up years, no one could get him off whichever was his favorite mount of the month. Ponies. Then full-grown horses when his parents thought him ready. The whole family joked at times, "He even rode a cow!"

And then it became his life's work. He loved training young horses. Watching them catch on to things he had patiently taught them. He could see it in their eyes, something no one else saw. The comprehension of a new task or trick, the trust they developed with their master. Everyone said he had the gift. And then he had moved to town and away from what he thought would be his life's work.

Travis looked forward to teaching his son to ride and felt sure Wyatt had the horse gene as well. He sure loved the donkey and all the different animals at the Christmas Open House. What a good time they had. But then Wyatt got sick, which scared Travis to death. If anything ever happened to his boy...Don't go there, he caught himself. His mother used to recite a Bible verse—*take every thought captive*—in other words, think positive thoughts, don't let your mind go down a rabbit trail or along a scary path. Easier said than done sometimes.

Wyatt had come home from the hospital earlier this week and was getting better and better each day. The doctor had told them it would take eight to ten days to fully recuperate from the RSV virus. Anyone could see the little guy was nearly a hundred percent. And now Christmas was almost here which only accelerated Wyatt's enthusiasm. Surely it would be an over-the-top celebration for the Olsen clan. If only Destynee were here. *Take every thought captive*. Travis might need to pinch himself to remember.

"Travis!" his brother Nathan called to him. He was on horseback, too, and rode closer. "What're you doin' up here?"

"Just thinking. And looking over the place." He turned to nod hello to his brother. "How'd you find me?"

"Gabe was up all night. I decided to visit the folks so he and Indya could get a nap. Mom said you rode out over an hour ago."

"And you knew where to find me."

"You do realize it's Sunday, don't you? I don't think Angie needs you to work," Nathan said.

"And I know you know that ranching is seven days a week." He grinned. "I'm not actually working. Checking the fence line, but we always do that. Mostly, I'm just thinking."

"Praying? Thanking God for protecting Wyatt? I am glad to hear he's out of the hospital."

"Yes, big brother. That, too. I'm super grateful that Wyatt is nearly all the way back to being a bubbly, full of energy, wild little boy."

"As he should be. He is a pistol. That's for sure."

"A son of a gun, right?" They both laughed. And walked their horses side by side towards the fence line.

"What else is on your mind, Travis? You know we all can see it on your face."

"What can you see?"

Nathan hesitated. “Heartache. Loneliness. Sometimes anger.”

“In the hospital I made up my mind.” He hesitated, not sure if he was ready to share, but went ahead. “If I have to do this parenting thing alone, then I’ll be the best father to Wyatt that anyone ever could be. And I’m okay with that. I need to just focus on my son.”

Nathan was quiet as he stared at his brother. The horses ambled on farther. Travis loved the easy rhythm, the peace that filled his body and soul. There was nothing better than being on horseback.

“Travis?”

“Yeah?”

“I respect the notion that you are a married man now who can make decisions for your family, and not just my little brother, but I’ve got a few questions for you.”

“Okay.”

“Do you love Destynee? Do you want to be with her the rest of your life? Do you want her to be at your side to raise Wyatt and watch him grow?”

Travis gulped and cautiously glanced at his brother. He didn’t really want to talk about all this. He had tried to make his peace with it.

“Well? Do you?” Nathan persisted.

“I guess so.” Travis’s voice was nearly a whisper, lost on the wind that was picking up. His answer was so less than what he actually wanted. It seemed pathetic at best.

“You need to own it and take control of the life you want. Communication is key to a successful marriage. I learned that the hard way. Take control.”

“You’re so bossy. Just like Angie.”

Nathan turned in the saddle, easing into a wide smile. “That’s my job. Just one more question, little brother.”

“What?” He sneered at Nathan.

"Tell me, why are you still here?"

"What do you mean? I'm checking fence."

Nathan rolled his eyes skyward. "I mean, Travis, why aren't you on your way to getting your wife? And bringing her back home."

Travis thought about the day his wife got in the car with her mother and drove away. She had made her decision at that moment. He had missed his chance to tell her then how he felt.

"I can't just make her come home. It's her career. I don't want to stand in her way. I can take care of Wyatt. We're doing just fine."

"That's on her then, but at least you'll have a clear conscience. You can't force her to do something she doesn't want to do, but is this the best way for your family to live? Is it an ideal situation? Apart? That's like two single people doing their own thing. Don't let stubborn pride stand in your way, Travis. If Indya was in a different city, you can be sure I'd go after her. She's my wife, mother of my son."

Travis's head hurt. His heart hurt. He wasn't sure what to do. He gritted his teeth, his mind whirling at the hard choices he had to make.

Nathan was forceful. "How many months has this gone on? Pretty soon you'll lose it all if you don't make a move."

"I can't just storm into her life."

"It's *your* life, together with her! Now where will she be tonight? How many hours will it take you to drive there?"

"I dunno. I never had a chance to look, but she has a website now."

They stopped to open the gate into ranch headquarters.

"Can you get a signal on your phone yet?" Nathan jumped to the ground to relatch the gate.

"Maybe so," Travis said as he pulled it from his pocket. He tapped in her name and there her website was, top of the list. A banner stretched across the top, blinking in colorful lights and announcing her next show.

"Nashville." One part of him was so proud, the other part knew she was gone. There was no turning away from that type of exposure.

"Nashville? That's huge, Travis!"

Travis glanced at his brother, not realizing he had said the city out loud. They dismounted and unsaddled the horses. Nathan was a bundle of energy.

"You've got to go support her and then talk. You two have got to talk. You'll have to fly. Let's get back to the house. I'll help you book a flight. I'll even drive you to the airport. And I am *not* taking no for an answer."

Travis wasn't exactly sure what just happened. But Nathan took charge as he usually did. And Travis didn't really mind. It was time he made a move and went after the girl of his dreams. For the second time.

40
TRAVIS

THE EARLY BIRD FLIGHT WAS UNDERWAY FROM the Texas Panhandle. Travis should arrive in time to rent a car, check into a motel, and find the café where Destynee would be singing. He had to change planes in Dallas, and then on to Nashville. According to the colorful banner on her website, the show started that evening. He should have plenty of time to get a ticket and find his seat. When she walked on stage, he would be there, supporting his talented wife and then he would ask her to come home.

She'd have to talk to him after the show. No more ignoring texts or phone messages. This would go down face to face. Big brother Nathan was right. Travis had to do this. At least she would know where he stood and what he wanted for their future. What he had always wanted. His Destynee back.

The sad thing about his life was he had no idea what her reaction was going to be. Did he not even know her anymore? And that realization hurt the most of all. How had he let his marriage reach this point?

From under the seat, he pulled out a small carryall and fumbled around inside for the off chance he might have remembered to pack antacid tablets. Instead, he found a package of oatmeal cookies and peanut butter crackers. His mother's doing no doubt. He smiled, choosing the crackers. The protein would hold him over until the next meal, whenever that might be.

He told the flight attendant coffee, but then regretted his order. The last thing he needed were more jittery nerves. His head felt like it was about to explode as it was. Staring out the window, he watched the crop circles that dotted the flat Llano Estacado. Clumps of trees gave hints of farmhouses, and then they flew over the breaks, where the unbroken table lands turned into the hills and trees of central Texas. That's when he saw it. A thunder-cloud rolling dark and ominous on the horizon.

He had practiced over and over in his mind what he wanted to say to Destynee. He wasn't whole without her. She was his world. Travis and Wyatt could not be a family without her in their lives. There had to be a way they could all be together. Maybe a family camper? He could save every cent and with what she made singing they might be able to make payments on some type of vehicle that would get them down the road. His mother-in-law could follow in her car, or not go at all. With him along, Destynee wouldn't be alone on the road.

The captain's voice sounded scratchy but the message was clear. "We'll be diverting around the storm and we've put the seatbelt sign on. It may get a little bumpy."

Travis frowned. He'd miss the connecting flight for sure.

~

THE LANDING WAS smooth under a light rain. Travis bolted as soon as the door was opened and before most of the other passengers had time to unbuckle and stand. Making his way through the crowd to the next gate he paused a minute to read the lighted board. Delayed. At least he didn't miss it. His phone beeped but he didn't have time to read the message or reply. He just wanted to get to the right gate, and hopefully make it on board. Stress gnawed at his stomach.

He checked the airline app on his phone. Everything seemed okay except for the delay. He only had four more gates to go before he made it to the one he needed. Thirty-two. He could see the sign up ahead. His phone beeped again, and this time he pulled it from his pocket to glance at the screen, but kept walking.

"No," he muttered under his breath. Flight canceled due to mechanical issues. They had booked him on the first flight out in the morning, but he wasn't defeated yet. Walking up to the counter, he smiled although he felt far from being friendly. "I need to get to Nashville today. Are there any other flights?"

The agent shook her head no before she even looked up. "We are full, and we're trying to reroute all of the passengers from this flight."

"Can you just take a look, please?"

He texted Nathan. *In Dallas. How many miles to Nashville? Might drive it.*

He'd already flown to the middle of the country. It couldn't be that much farther to Tennessee. His phone rang. He started not to answer because he wanted to find a rental car desk first, but changed his mind. "Yeah."

"You can't drive. What happened?"

Hearing Nathan's voice helped calm him a bit. But

not much. "Cancelled. I'm not going anywhere until early tomorrow morning."

"Aren't you at an airport?"

"Yeah. I'm still in Dallas."

"Aren't there other airlines at that airport?"

Travis felt like an idiot. There was no rule he had to fly on the same airline he started with. "You're a genius."

Nathan laughed. "You're just stressed. Hang on. Let me check. Indya is looking, too. I'll call you right back."

Travis took a deep breath to get it together before he tried talking to the attendant again. "What about another airline that can get me to Nashville? Or even Atlanta?" As big as the Atlanta airport was, he could surely get a connection from there, if he couldn't fly direct from where he was.

"You'll have to use the kiosk for that, sir."

It was obvious they were not going to be of any help, so Travis decided to let his brother figure it out. In the meantime, he'd find some food for his rumbling stomach. The only problem was this international airport was huge.

HE HAD JUST TAKEN one bite of a cheeseburger when his phone buzzed.

"Nathan. Tell me you found something."

"There's a flight leaving in one hour. Listen closely because I've worked out the route for you. You need to find the airport shuttle."

"Hang on." Travis wrapped up his burger, slung his bag over one shoulder, and hightailed it in the direction of the arrow and signs for the train.

"Go on," he said.

"You are currently in Building B, and you need to ride the train towards Building E. And then to gate twenty. You'll need to stop at a kiosk when you get to the right building and check in for your boarding pass. Your ticket is paid for. Good luck, brother."

"Nathan, I owe you one."

"No, you don't. Go find your Destynee and bring her back. The family is counting on you."

41
TRAVIS

DECEMBER IN NASHVILLE. IT FELT WARMER than Texas, which was a good thing because he had forgotten to grab his jean jacket. Wished he could be here under better circumstances. He had always been a country music fan, and even missed playing his guitar. He hadn't picked it up since Wyatt was born.

Travis didn't have time to rent a car or check in to a motel, so he took an Uber to the Café. The driver was extra friendly, providing his take on the best places to eat and the most popular sights. Neon lights lined both sides of the street, clever names for the bars highlighted by blinking guitars in a myriad of colors mixed with holiday decoration. The driver stopped the car along the curb.

"Stardust Café, right across the street. Hope you find what you're looking for." The Uber driver offered, which seemed strange under the circumstances.

"Thanks, man." Travis nodded and got out of the car.

His hopes were dashed when he saw the crowd that had already formed at the door. Might as well get in line and hope for the best, and that is exactly what he did, except the people weren't just waiting along the sidewalk in front of the Café. The line wrapped around along the side street, too. With his hands in his pockets, he ambled past the crowd and found a place at the very back. Dead last. Great.

If he hadn't taken his hat off to wipe the sweat from his brow, he probably wouldn't have seen his mother-in-law strutting past towards the front door.

"Julee Rae!" He ran after her. It was just like her to use the main entrance, moving through the crowd with a haughty arrogance like she was somebody instead of entering through the back stage door. She liked being seen and heard, thriving on the attention.

Spinning around on high-heeled boots, the bright smile on her face quickly disappeared into a deep frown the moment she saw him. He was too close by then. She couldn't escape.

"What are *you* doing here?" She gave him a nasty frown.

"I need to see Destynee."

"You need to leave. I'm calling security." She shook her head as though he were a lunatic.

"She is my wife. I have every right to talk to her."

"My daughter cannot be bothered with you at this point in time. This is her big break. She cannot see you or even know that you're here. It may jeopardize everything we've worked for."

"I'm not here to stop her. I just need to see her." Pleading, he tried his best to be civil with his mother-in-law.

"That is impossible. She's already backstage."

"Just tell me one thing. Why hasn't she answered my texts or returned my phone calls?"

"You are a distraction. She can't have that now."

"Her son was in the hospital. Your grandson. She needs to know about him."

The look of surprise that crossed Julee Rae's face and then the avoidance of his eyes explained everything. He never imagined his mother-in-law being capable of sabotaging her own daughter's marriage.

Rage built up inside his gut, and he clenched his hands into fists. "You! I don't know how, but you must've erased my texts and deleted the recent call list. It was *you*." That last word he spit out through tight jaws, as though the word was so vile, he could hardly say it out loud.

She pretended innocence with a blank look on her face, but he saw it. Just for a split second he saw the guilt that passed through her eyes. They stood frozen in time. Glaring at each other. He knew security would never allow him into the show as long as she had anything to say about it.

"Don't you dare come near her, or I will have you arrested." Julee Rae turned and walked as fast as she could towards the front entrance.

"Aren't you even going to ask if your grandson is okay?" The question was aimed at her back and by the time he finished asking it, he was standing there talking to the air. A few people gave him curious glances.

Travis had never been a name dropper, but he was going to start now. If Destynee had become as famous as everybody kept telling him, then surely her husband wielded some clout, too.

He marched past the crowd and stopped in front of the two bouncers that met him with a glare. He assumed it was a glare because they remained motionless behind reflective sunglasses, with forearms as big around as his thigh.

"What you want, cowboy?"

"I'm Travis Olsen. Destynee is my wife. I'm running late. I should have been here earlier, but my flight out of Dallas was cancelled. Can I see her?"

"See who?"

"Destynee."

"Get to the back of the line."

"She's my wife."

The bulging muscles were not going to move out of the way.

"Get to the end of the line! We've been waiting for two hours." A voice shouted from the crowd. Others grumbled.

He walked back towards from where he had come from, around the side of the building to find his spot again, when he saw the alley. He'd just wait her out. With this many people, he knew she wouldn't exit out the front door.

The voices died down as the line moved closer to the entrance, and soon he was sitting on an upturned crate in the silent darkness. He could hear the band warming up. The occasional twang of a steel guitar, and once the unmistakable sound of a saxophone.

The alley was suddenly illuminated by light as the back door slowly opened. A girl slipped out and the door slammed before he could see her face. She wore white boots, a black leather mini skirt, and a silky white blouse that shimmered with fringe in the dim alley light. A cascade of blonde hair hung to her waist from under a cowboy hat that had a huge white feather on the brim. She leaned against the side of the building; her eyes closed but the streetlights reflected the tear tracks on her cheeks. A sob escaped from her lips. Her perfume smelled familiar.

"Destynee?" He walked towards the woman slowly, his heart pounding out of his chest, hoping against all odds that this might be his wife. *Good Lord, if you're watching, I could sure use a break.*

42
DESTYNEE

SIX DAYS UNTIL CHRISTMAS

Her name floated on the breeze, ever so gently like in a dream. And if she had been dreaming, there was no doubt that Travis was the one who uttered it. But that's impossible. The stress must be getting to her. More than she had realized.

She didn't have a tissue or anything to wipe her wet eyes and nose, so she pulled out the tail end of her shirt and used that. They'd have to redo her stage makeup, but she didn't care. She tucked it back in before anybody noticed.

"My Destynee."

There it was again. And something blocked the glaring streetlight. She raised her head and opened her eyes, suspecting that she had finally gone mad. It was a nightmare. She was about to be attacked by a cowboy who looked exactly like her husband. Panic set in for a split second, but she would have recognized that old cowboy hat anywhere. She sighed, not believing her eyes.

He leaned closer and wrapped his arms around her before claiming her mouth. She didn't resist. He stopped to give her air, and then a familiar face pressed his warm lips on hers again.

"Travis?" Instead of answering, he kissed her for the third time. This time deeper, with a longing that made her want to weep. She melted into him. His scent, the hardness of his chest, and as those muscled arms surrounded her, she knew this was where she belonged. She would never turn her back on this part of her life ever again. They stood there locked in an embrace for the longest time. She didn't care how long.

"What are you doing here?" She smiled. He did, too. His hair was longer since the last time she had seen him, just past his shirt collar. The same hat, starched jeans, and the same smile that made her knees go weak.

"I heard about a singer who was making her debut at the Stardust Café. Heard she'd be worth the trip to hear." He reached a hand to her face and gently wiped the moisture away that clung to her cheeks.

"You came all that way to see me?"

"Yes, ma'am, I did."

Her smile widened and then her face took on an unpleasant twist. Anger replaced the love she had felt only seconds before and she shoved him.

"Our son was in the hospital and you never told me? How dare you."

"I tried—"

She cut him off. "Not one word. Not one phone call."

"Wait. How did you know about—"

"You ripped my heart out, Travis Olsen, and I will never forgive you. How dare you keep my son from me. How dare you keep secrets. I should have been at his bedside. My precious baby. I could have—" And then she doubled over with sobs.

Travis put his hands around her arms and pulled her to him. "I swear. I tried."

She managed to control her emotions and then said, "I needed to be there. He'll never understand why his mother wasn't there."

He stood stock-still with a grief stricken look on his face.

"Is he...okay?" She muttered through her tears.

"He is fine. It was a mild case of RSV. They kept him for a few days under an oxygen tent."

"Thank, God." She closed her eyes and then the anger resurged again. "And you moved. Took my son with you, and didn't tell me about that either."

"Listen—"

"I don't know you anymore." She poked a finger into his chest. "You are not the man I married. Who are you?"

His eyes turned stony with anger. "Who am I? You have no right to ask me that."

She gasped and backed up. His jaw tightened and he balled his hands into fists as he tried to calm his temper. She could see the struggle in his face.

"Let's talk about you. Miniskirts and boots. My wife's thighs pasted all over the internet. Your shirt unbuttoned down to your navel. Who are *you*?"

She opened her mouth in shock. "My shirt was not unbuttoned that far. How dare you accuse me of something I would never do."

They glared at each other for a few seconds, and then he gave her a questioning look.

"How did you know about the hospital? How did you know we moved out of your mother's house? Believe me,

I tried to contact you."

"I saw it on your sister's posts. Along with picture from the Wild Cow Ranch Open House. I can't believe how much I'm missing of my son's life."

"You got that right."

"And I came to Dixon to find you," she said. That took him totally by surprise. "I couldn't find you in town at mother's house, so I drove out to the ranch. No one was home."

"We must have been at the hospital with Wyatt. Why didn't you call me?"

"You stopped answering, Travis." And then she lowered her voice to a whisper. "You never returned my calls, so I figured why bother. I drove all night to Dixon so that I could talk to you face-to-face."

"You never returned any of my messages either. I came here to tell you that your son misses you. We want you home. Yes, you're missing a lot, and you already know it. I also came to hear you sing. You will always have my support in whatever you want to do."

"You're too late."

He backed away. "You've already gone on? I missed it?" A glazed look of misery spread over his face.

"You haven't missed anything. I'm not singing. I'm leaving with you. Let's go." She tugged his hand but he pulled her back.

Surprise flickered in his eyes, and then his smile broadened with joy. His arms wrapped around her in a tight hug. He chuckled. But then he stepped away, a deep frown creased his forehead. "You have to sing. I'm not holding you back."

"No. I'm not doing it. I'm done with this. My talent is God-given, and I feel blessed every day to sing in front of people. I should be able to use it the way that makes me happy, for His glory. I want this to be fun again."

"You were meant for this moment. You have to share your gift with the world. This could be the break that shoots you to super stardom." The last part he whispered, without much enthusiasm.

"I have dreamed about singing in Nashville my entire life and now I realize I can't. Look at me." She waved her hand at the outfit she was wearing. "This is not who I am." Panic rose in her chest. Again. At the thought of what she had to do to make everybody happy.

The door pushed open with a force and Destynee had to step back out of the way. She heard her mother's voice. "Call security!"

Julee Rae exploded into the alley and stopped in front of Travis. Lucius followed close behind, and the door slammed shut. She pointed a finger at him. "If you and your brat get anywhere close to my daughter, I will have you arrested."

"Mother?" Destynee saw the shock and horror on her mother's face as she turned to look behind her. "Sweetheart. I can explain."

43
DESTYNEE

DESTYNEE LOOKED AT JULEE RAE AND THEN AT Travis. Even in the dim light of the alley, she could see the distress in her mother's eyes and the condemnation when she looked at her son-in-law. Her mouth spread into a thin-lipped smile.

"This must be the husband." His voice heavy with sarcasm and disgust, Lucius gave Travis a once-over from head to toe. Destynee wanted to punch him.

"Mother, that brat is my son. Your grandson. Did you know Wyatt had been in the hospital?"

Her mother did not answer. There was no surprise on her face, and she couldn't even fake sincere concern.

"You knew." Destynee walked to stand in front of Travis who was facing Julee Rae.

"What has he told you?" she haughtily asked.

"What do you mean?"

"Don't believe anything he tells you. He makes up lies about me. He has been trying to derail your career from the moment you started dating. I knew he would ruin your life, and then you had to get pregnant. I saved your career, no thanks to him."

"What could he possibly be telling me about you, Mother?" Destynee glared at her, and then it all became clear. "You erased my texts and phone calls. Why would you do that?"

She screamed that last part. All of the pent-up emotion, sadness, and confusion came to the forefront in her brain, and she realized one person was the reason. The one person who should have had her back was using her and manipulating her to become something she wasn't. Her own mother had almost ruined her marriage and kept her from her son.

"That's enough. Everyone just calm down. Destynee, let's get you back inside. You have to do this." Lucius opened the door, holding it wide.

"No, I don't." Destynee crossed her arms over her chest.

"There have been a lot of people who have worked tirelessly to get you to this point in your career." Julee Rae gripped her daughter's arms and shook her. "You will not destroy this for me. Tell him to leave."

"He is my husband. He has a right to be here."

She had never seen her mother this angry.

"I am a good manager." A sob escaped her lips. "Every sacrifice I've made, every hour I've spent begging people to let you sing, every demo tape and deejay I've talked to. It's all been for us. This what we've always wanted."

"This is what YOU wanted, Mother."

"But this is the moment. All of our dreams could come true, if you don't blow it."

Travis stepped closer and gently removed Julee Rae's

hands from his wife. He placed a hand on Destynee's cheek. "She's right. You have to do this."

She hesitated. Looking from one to the other, turmoil bubbling up inside her until she thought she might scream. Three against one. The odds were not in her favor. She looked into the eyes of her husband, trying to hold back the tears.

"We'll make this work, but together. From now on, if you're on the road then Wyatt and I will be there, too. If you want to stay home, then we'll do that. We will live anywhere you want, but we do it as a family."

"You would do that for me?"

"I will do anything for you and Wyatt. For us. He needs a mother who can watch him grow and help him walk. Sing him to sleep every night. And I need you. This family doesn't work without you, Destynee." He paused, the expression in his eyes pleading and sad. "You are my breath. Did you know that?"

"Yes. I've known it since the first time I saw you at the county rodeo. You haven't given me a moment's peace since."

He laughed. "Together. That's the only way this will work."

"Together." She nodded in agreement.

"I love you, my beautiful wife."

"I love you, too, Travis. With all my heart." She lifted her chin, meeting her mother's icy glare. "But I have to do things my way."

She removed the feather monstrosity from the top of her head and handed it to Lucius. "I'm not wearing this."

"That's a $10,000 custom-made western hat. It's your signature piece! I can't return that."

From her pocket she produced a pink scrunchy and

pulled her massive curls back into a ponytail. Lucius gasped.

"That is not the image we want to present." He protested between thin lips.

"You're fired," she said. Lucius gave her a look of total shock. "But I want you to know that when I figure out what type of singing career I want you'll be the first person I call. Thanks for all you did."

He actually smiled at that and they hugged. Without saying another word to her mother, she grabbed Travis's hand, spun on her boot heels, and walked back inside.

BACK STAGE WAS CONTROLLED CHAOS. She could feel the nervous energy that only came from performers. She loved that feeling and she loved being a part of this world, and she loved her son and husband, too. There had to be a way to strike a balance. *I can't do this without you, Lord.*

A group of siblings were singing on stage, their voices melded into perfect harmony. She didn't speak to anyone, just forged through the bustle dragging Travis along behind her. She found her guitar case leaned against a dressing table and removed the instrument. After a brief glance in the lighted mirror, she opened her makeup case. Instead of applying more she found a cloth and wiped some of it off.

She turned to look at her husband. "Wish me luck."

He kissed her lips. "Good luck, my love."

A man with a clipboard stopped behind her. "Destynee? You're on in three, two, one."

She heard her name from the stage. The audience clapped. She walked out into the middle of the crowd and sat down on the stool, rested her guitar on her lap, and strummed a few notes to get her fingers warmed up. She raised her head and smiled.

"Hello. My name is Des—" She glanced into the wings and saw her husband watching, beaming with pride. "I'm Travis's wife and our son's name is Wyatt. I'd like to sing a song for y'all."

EPILOGUE

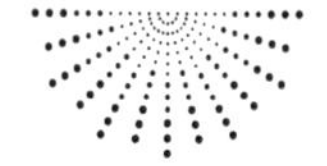

CHRISTMAS EVE

THE CHRISTIAN CHURCH IN DIXON, TEXAS could have been on the front of a Christmas card. Destynee stopped in the middle of the sidewalk to admire the image. The light filtering through the elaborate stained-glass windows duplicated the colors on the white ground.

From the pristine white exterior, a steeple towered above the roof line as a beacon of hope and peace. The building was one of the oldest in the county. Surrounded by bushes, planted and maintained by devoted volunteers, the missing leaves were replaced by fluffy clumps of white. Bright red bows on evergreen wreaths decorated the wooden front doors. Someone had draped the lower half of a blue spruce with twinkle lights. This night a gentle dusting of snow fluttered in the air, giving a clean slate to the land. And the people.

Travis stopped next to her and slung an arm over her shoulders. "Are you ready for this?"

She laughed. "I was born ready for this."

"That's my girl." He kissed her cheek and then averted his gaze back to the view. "I'm glad you're here tonight. I wasn't sure if you would be." His voice broke.

"Why are you two standing in the cold? Let's get this baby inside." Grace brushed past them carrying a bundle that looked more like a wad of clothes than their son. Skip followed close behind, a twinkle in his eye as he gave them a wink.

"I wish mother could be here." A deep sadness washed over her, taking away the peace she had felt only seconds before.

"I know you do, babe. You have to do what's right for you." Travis placed a warm hand in the small of her back and they walked towards the light and warmth. The pressure of him beside her gave her courage.

Not sure where her mother, Julee Rae, was this evening. And she was sorry for that. They had parted ways on a battlefield. It was as if God had given Destynee the strength to hold her ground as well as new eyes to see. For the first time in her life, she had seen the anger and jealousy consuming Julee Rae like a poison. She would pray for her mother and hope for a reconciliation in the future.

But for now, she had to concentrate on what God had bestowed upon her. And keep her new life clean, holy, positive, and uplifting for all those around her. She wanted to safeguard Wyatt and teach him to live a good life, to become a godly man. She wanted to be a good wife. And she now understood that she could be all of these things and stay true to her music, too.

Tomorrow morning, Wyatt would open his presents under the Christmas tree and she would be there. She could hardly wait to see his face light up when he finds the giant stuffed horse that his daddy got for him. Travis had told her about the shopping trip with his mother. One day she knew Travis would get him a real horse. And she would always pray for his safety and that of their whole family. There was no guarantee of course for perfect happiness. Not in this world.

She knew there would be many ups and downs. Even tragedies and losses. But still, she was grateful. Thankful to God for restoring her marriage and her little family. And she knew nothing could ever divide them again.

Inside, while Travis settled in the pew with his family, Destynee walked to the front to sit in a chair behind the pulpit along with the rest of the choir. She might consider joining them full-time in the new year, but for now she would only be singing one or two songs that the pastor had requested. After that she'd be able to sit with her family. She smoothed her green velvet dress and was so glad it wasn't one of those glittery costumes her mother used to choose for her. The only spotlight she wanted now was the flickering of holy candlelight.

Life was definitely a roller coaster ride as people sometimes said. Ups and downs, twists and turns. Unpredictable. Scary at times when it headed for the depths of despair. And wonderfully thrilling as it climbed towards a breathtaking mountaintop of joy. It helped if you had someone you loved beside you to experience it all together.

Destynee was amazed at how different she felt. Emotionally, spiritually, even physically. Like a brand-new person. Tension and confusion had all fallen to the wayside. She could finally breathe. And she felt content. Calm. This kind of life she could do. All the jumbled pieces had neatly fallen into place. She prayed they would never get out of whack again.

God had done this. She knew it had to be Him because however hard she and Travis had attempted to figure things out, on their own, it never worked out. It had been the opposite of peace. Their lives had been filled with heartache, misunderstanding, and almost a tearing apart of their marriage. If they had stayed on that path, she was sure it would have not only destroyed their lives for years to come but also that of her sweet son.

Thank God. Thank Him for saving us from ourselves.

Destynee understood that she and Travis had each found their true path that God had planned for them all along. He still let them make their own choices. They had free will. But He always wanted the best for them and their job was to follow their destiny towards Him. Song lyrics began to swirl in her head. Maybe one day she could share that knowledge through song.

As everyone settled in their seats, the pastor walked up to the podium, pausing for a moment to let the talking fade. He held up both hands. "Thank you for joining us. Ladies and gentlemen, we have a special blessing this Christmas Eve. A lot of us know this young lady and have watched her career skyrocket. Now she has returned to Dixon and we couldn't be happier to welcome her home. With the voice of an angel, here is Destynee Olsen."

She was glad he used her last name. For that was who she really was. Travis's wife. Wyatt's mother. Next to them and in the row behind were every member of the Olsen clan, all come home for Christmas. She belonged with them. Her big family.

A little voice sounded. "Mama", then a giggle. She waved at Wyatt when she stood which made him giggle again. Sitting on his daddy's lap so he could see better, he looked so sweet in the little suit his grandmother had found for him, complete with a red bow tie.

To the sound of polite applause, Destynee walked to stand behind the podium, and then stepped to the side to pull the guitar strap over her head. "I think y'all can hear me without that microphone."

A small congregation, all familiar faces, everyone smiled at her. Such a contrast from a performance hall of a thousand strangers.

She nodded at the pianist and then closed her eyes allowing the organ music to flow through her veins, the Holy Spirit's peace easing her mind and making her feel certain that she had made the right decision. She was going to focus on gospel music. All the hard work, lonely nights, arguments with her mother floated away until all that was left was this moment. This was where her heart was happiest.

The sight of her husband and son on the front row with giant smiles on their faces brought tears to her eyes.

Destynee sang the first verse soft and reverent, "I heard the bells on Christmas day, their old familiar carols play."

The congregation remained spellbound as she sang. She sensed their energy and when the choir joined in, the song rose to the next level. Her powerful voice rang clear and true, and as the last notes hung in the space, the sound waves reflected back from the walls. The applause was delayed, as if everyone was afraid to break the reverence of the evening.

This would be the Christmas Eve that she will remember for the rest of her life.

ACKNOWLEDGMENTS

The Rafter O Series would not be possible if it were not for the support and hard work of our publisher, CKN Christian Publishing and Wolfpack Publishing. Authors rely on a team with knowledge of the publishing industry and methods for the best ways to find readers. Wolfpack is exceptional on all counts.

Special thanks also go to Micki Fuhrman Milom who gave us an invaluable insight to country music industry. Thanks, Micki, for your willingness to share your experiences and answer our questions. *Finding My Destynee* is all the better because of you. I highly recommend Micki's latest collection of award-winning songs, including her "Westbound" album. Go to www.mickifuhrmanmusic.com.

Thanks to my co-author, Denise. We never imagined we had so many stories in us.

And most importantly, thank you romance fans. I hope you enjoy reading about the Olsen Family. Please connect with us online and give us your feedback by posting a starred review. Your efforts go a long way in helping other readers find our books.

~Natalie Bright

As always, many thanks to my co-author and dear friend, Natalie Bright. She is creative, patient, and great to work with. It has been a fun and educational journey.

Thanks to many others for their support and encouragement: family and friends foremost, the Western Writers of America, and Wolfpack Publishing and CKN Christian Publishing.

We appreciate our faithful readers and pray God will bless you abundantly.

~Denise F. McAllister

IF YOU LIKE THIS, YOU MAY ALSO ENJOY: MAVERICK HEART

WILD COW RANCH BOOK ONE

FROM HORSE SHOWING IN GEORGIA TO RIDING THE RANGE IN TEXAS – A TALE OF COURAGE AND FINDING FAITH.

Carli Jameson is used to being on her own – abandoned by her mother as an infant – all she's ever wanted is to feel like she belongs. She has had no choice except to be strong and independent, but now, can she learn to trust God to be her partner?

Georgia girl, Carli Jameson, inherits a Texas cattle ranch from grandparents she never knew. After much thought, she makes the courageous decision to pack up her life and move to Texas to run the ranch. She forges ahead into a new life filled with uncertainty and along the way discovers a ranching community that becomes the family she never had.

Independent, ambitious and smart, Carli has always been careful with her heart, except for the one time she thought she had found her soul mate and true love. He proved her wrong, and she vowed never to jump into a romantic relationship that easily again. When Carli drives away from her life in Georgia, no looking back, she intends to stick with her vow and not fall into any sweet romances, especially with a Texas cowboy.

Can a fresh start erase the troubles of her past?

AVAILABLE NOW

ABOUT NATALIE BRIGHT

With roots firmly planted in the Texas Panhandle, Natalie Bright grew up obsessed with the Wild West and making up stories. The small farming community where she lived gave her a belief in hard-working, genuine people and a firm foundation of faith. She is the author of books for kids and adults, as well as numerous articles.

This author and blogger writes about small town heroes with complicated pasts and can-do attitudes, who navigate life's crazy misfortunes with humor and happy endings.

ABOUT DENISE F. MCALLISTER

Lovers of the West can be born in the most unlikely of places. For Denise F. McAllister, her start was in Miami, Florida, surrounded by beaches and the Everglades.

But the marvels of television transported her to stories of the West—*Bonanza, Gunsmoke, The Virginian, Big Valley, The Lone Ranger, Daniel Boone,* and many others—that she fondly recalls watching with her brother every Saturday morning.

After being in the working world for some years, Denise decided to apply her life experience and study for her B.A. in communications and M.A. in professional writing.

To this day, her faith is important to her, and she loves to write about characters' journeys as they navigate real-world challenges. She prays that readers will enjoy her books, but—more importantly—experience a blessed connection with their Creator and Heavenly Father.

Made in the USA
Middletown, DE
21 October 2022